MAN DOWN

SEALS OF SHADOW FORCE: SPY DIVISION,
BOOK 3

MISTY EVANS

Man Down, SEALs of Shadow Force Series

Spy Division, Book 3

Copyright © 2019 Misty Evans

ISBN: 978-1-94686-07-5

Print: 978-1-948686-27-3

Cover Art by Fanderclai Design

Formatting by Beach Path Publishing, LLC

Editing by Elizabeth Neal, Patricia Essex

Please Note

To Mark, you had me at hello

"And as every spy knows, common enemies are how allies always begin." ~ Ally Carter

Murphy is right. What can go wrong, will go wrong, and at the worst possible moment.

"Aidan."

The voice came from faraway, floating through the fog in his brain. Sweat coated his body, his mouth dry as cotton.

"Mr. McNamara."

Fucking black death prison, deep in the heart of Russia, run by inmates rather than law enforcement. It would kill him, like so many others, he was sure.

I won't give Vaslov the satisfaction.

Something poked his arm. He lay still, his body so heavy he would've sworn he was paralyzed. Maybe he was.

"Aidan!" *Poke, poke, poke.* "Wake up!"

The thin wire holding him together, snapped. He didn't have time to think, his body reacting, dragging him out of the nightmare with rapid speed.

Bam, in the blink of an eye he came off the bed, grabbed the hand of the person poking him, and now had said person on the floor, his larger body hulking over them.

A woman screamed and the sound cut off mid-vocalization, a muffled gurgling noise following. He rammed a knee into his assailant's stomach, one hand pinning a wrist to the floor, the other around their neck.

"Aidan!" Someone yelled from his left. "Boss, it's me. Me and *Megan*! Take it easy. We're not here to hurt you."

He blinked away the sweat and nightmare, his eyes focusing enough to see and *aww shit.* This wasn't good.

"Let her go, boss," he heard the familiar voice say. "You don't want to do this."

He couldn't seem to get enough air in his lungs, a crushing vise tightening around his chest. His head pounded, he couldn't swallow. *Where am I? How did I get free of my shackles?*

The only answer that came was the cold bite of metal against his temple, the calculating sound of a hammer being pulled back. "You're not in Russia anymore, McNamara. You're in Texas. You're free, not in some goddamn prison. Now, wake the fuck up before you do something you'll regret."

One quick movement and he could disarm the man holding a gun to his head. Another, and he could kill him.

The woman he held pinned to the floor gave a squeak.

The fog in his brain lifted, the grip around his chest released, and he found himself staring down into the terrified eyes of Megan Caines, his boss's personal assistant. Everything came back to him in one fell swoop.

Scrambling backward, he lifted his hands in the air and glanced up to see Joey Tomas holding the gun on him as he reached down to help Ms. Caines to her feet.

"You okay, boss?" Joey asked as he shuffled Megan behind him. She coughed, rubbing her throat. "You with us now?"

The nightmare flashback still hung on the edges of his mind, like sleep in the corners of his eyes. Aidan sat on the edge of the bed, scrubbing his face with his hands. "Jesus, Megan. I'm so fucking sorry."

Joey pocketed the gun. "My fault. We knocked, but you didn't hear." He was close to six feet with dark hair and deeply tanned skin. Megan peeked over his shoulder, her generous heels giving her the ability to stay behind Joey's protective stance and stare at Aidan with wide eyes. "I know it's your day off, but we have a new arrival. Mr. DeMarco sent us to wake you. I should've done it alone."

Always dangerous to sneak up on him, especially when he was dead to the world. The PTSD was borderline these days, but still a constant shadow. Maybe if he hadn't been up until four AM working on the project hidden behind the false wall in his room, hadn't been so deeply asleep, he wouldn't have come out of it ready to kill someone.

He scrubbed his face. "Yeah, you should have." Joey knew about the PTSD, the nightmares. Knew about his past in that Russian hellhole. Not everything, of course, but enough.

Goddamnit, what if he'd hurt Megan? Killed her? He shut that line of thought down, knowing he'd figure out something later and apologize. "What's so urgent?"

"The new arrival is Protocol Alpha. Mr. DeMarco said you'd want to handle her security personally."

Aidan scratched the back of his head, squinting at the sunlight coming through the patio doors near the bed. He'd never hung blinds or curtains, and while he didn't have a fancy room overlooking the Gulf of Mexico, he could see a sliver of water from his balcony. "Who is she?"

Joey shook his head and shrugged. "No clue."

Megan, braver now, stepped out from behind her protector.

"She isn't on the guest list. There're plenty of rooms available, but not *Alpha* rooms. The suites are booked!"

The Gulf Breeze Spa and Resort sat on the pristine beaches of South Padre Island, Texas, and hosted a wide assortment of rich and famous visitors from all over the world. Actors, sports players, tycoons and billionaires...as well as a few spies and lowlifes like him.

Clients fit into one of three categories: alphas were the big whales, the billionaires and tycoons. Whoever this woman was, she obviously took it for granted they'd have one of their three famous penthouse suites available at a moment's notice.

Aidan sometimes resented that kind of person, one who had privileges he couldn't even dream of, and took the world for granted. Not that he had any desire to be rich or famous, but common decency and unselfishness didn't cost a damn thing in his world.

Doesn't matter what I think, or who I like and don't. This is the job. Besides, truth was, he was married to a very rich woman. "What time will she be here?"

Megan had gone to Aidan's closet and pulled it open. She flicked hangers, withdrawing a fresh suit to hang on the bathroom door. It annoyed him, her acting familiar with his stuff, and he shooed her away, snatching the suit before she made it to the bathroom door. There was only one woman, besides his mother, who'd he'd ever allowed to pick out his clothes.

Joey glanced at his watch. "DeMarco sent a limo to the airport to pick her up, but apparently she's driving. Should be here in eight minutes."

Great. "Give me five. I'll meet you downstairs."

JOEY WAS an efficient right-hand man and had Aidan's Protocol Alpha security team lined up at the front entrance by the time he made it downstairs. Megan had a personal maid and butler standing across from Joey and the team, along with the resort concierge and doorman.

It was as if they were lining up for a royal visitor. Hell, maybe they were. Wouldn't be the first time a member of a royal family spent the week with them. They usually brought their own security and even a chef. In that case, Aidan and his team played second fiddle, only lending backup when necessary. It was a pain to avoid the royal guards, but in a way, it was an easier gig than being in charge of some dickhead who thought his shit didn't stink.

Today's visitor was probably some monarch's daughter or sister, or maybe farther down the line—sister-in-law, cousin, girlfriend.

Didn't matter. The job was the job, no matter who showed up. An Alpha got top-line everything, from security to services at the spa. There were on-site trainers and physical therapists, cabanas down by the water with their own personal waiters, a variety of massages, body treatments, and health food available 24/7.

Martin DeMarco disembarked from the elevator, straightening his tie and smiling like the Cheshire Cat. He met Aidan's eyes and clapped him on the back as he walked by. "An early Christmas present," he said, winking at Aidan. "I can't believe she's here."

"Yes, sir," he said automatically, hoping Megan wouldn't report the morning's unfortunate incident to their mutual boss.

December was low season, the rich and famous spending the holidays with family and friends rather than at a ritzy health spa. A few here and there might despise the holidays or not have anyone to spend them with, and those misfits occasionally visited, but for the most part, December was spent prepping for the January rush, when even the Beta and Omega rooms were packed.

Through the wide expanse of glass windows, Aidan saw a slick, silver Maserati fly down the palm tree-lined drive. The woman behind the wheel had her window down, long, coppery strands blowing out the opening. Large, round sunglasses obscured her face, but as she drew to a stop at the front entrance, Aidan's stomach dropped.

This had to be part of the nightmare, a lingering aftereffect. A hallucination at the very least, brought on by too little sleep and too much alcohol before he'd crashed into bed in the wee hours of the morning.

Because God Almighty, the woman behind the wheel could *not* be who he thought it was.

DeMarco looked everyone over, nodded his approval, and made for the door, the doorman opening it for him. As the woman emerged from her car, the valet hurried from behind his small desk to offer a hand. She accepted, smiling at him before turning to face Martin, who threw his arms open wide—not just to welcome her, but to embrace her.

That's when Aidan knew—this was worse than a nightmare, than any PTSD flashback.

The woman wore a silky, red dress molded to her generous curves, and thick wedge heels that emphasized her sexy calves. The smile she gave Martin was that of a million-dollar model, her skin the color of the soft sand all around them.

Out under the canopy, Martin embraced her in a full bear hug, kissing her cheeks and calling her tender names. She laughed and spoke in low tones back to him, indulging his fatherly admonishments for not visiting sooner, for not warning him of her visit ahead of time.

Keeping an arm around her waist, he drew her past the decorated urns of flowers, vines, ferns, and the tiny lights and sparkling ribbons to emphasize a tasteful holiday decor, leading her inside.

Pulling himself up to this full six-foot, four inches, Aidan clamped his jaw shut to keep a myriad of curses he hadn't used since he was a SEAL from spilling out of his mouth as she removed her sunglasses and looked everyone over.

The staff smiled politely—except for Aidan's team—as Martin introduced them for the Alpha's approval. Security members did not smile. When they made it to the end of the line where Aidan stood, he kept his hand—the one he usually offered the guest—behind his back so he wouldn't strangle her.

Martin beamed, his grin still huge. "And of course, you remember my head of security."

The intense, golden-brown eyes that haunted his dreams as much as that damn Russian prison took their time rising up to meet his. "Hello, A."

Just like earlier, his mouth was too dry to speak, his head pounded. His chest felt the clamp of the vise around his ribs. A lifetime of memories flashed through him—Vegas, Camp Swampy, their last mission together when she'd nearly died. Drawing breath was out of the question.

Unfortunately, killing the woman he'd wedded, bedded, and saved from prison was too.

At his complete and utter silence, Bree DeMarco Russo-McNamara lifted one corner of her mouth and sighed. He knew that sound—that unending annoyance at him apparently still embedded in her system like it was her very DNA.

"Good to see you again, too, hubby" she murmured, grabbing her uncle's hand and strutting away.

STAY CALM; *the enemy wants confusion.*

FALLING in love is a fool's game, her mother always said. *Be smart.*

Five years. Five years since the first time she'd laid eyes on Aidan and he still took her breath away. As Bree turned her back on him to accompany Uncle Martin to the elevators, she kept her spine straight, chin lifted. She could not—*would not*—allow him to see the effect he still had on her.

The spa and hotel was the same as she remembered, marble floors, gold fixtures, crystal chandeliers. The receptionist, Candace, called a greeting from the front desk and gave her a large smile. Bree waved, acknowledging other nods and hellos from the staff as they passed. Most of them she'd known her whole life.

"We're so happy you're here," her uncle said, his accent so mild she could barely pick it up. "It's important to be with family at the holidays."

Family, in his mind, included her husband. The man whose eyes she could feel on her as they crossed the enormous foyer filled with cushy furniture and an atrium of green and flowering plants. Everything inside her wanted to turn and meet that molten gaze, to challenge the man who was not only her estranged husband, but her new assignment.

Be smart.

Easy for you to say, Mama. You and Daddy had a storybook romance.

Bree, on the other hand, had fallen for a Navy SEAL on leave in Vegas. One who'd shown up six months later at the CIA's domestic training center where she taught escape and invasion techniques.

She'd been contractually obligated to provide him with the best training possible. Didn't mean she hadn't tried to flunk him anyway.

Tried and failed.

The itch to look lingered, to maybe catch him unaware and see some emotion on his face.

No, she told yourself. *No looking back, no flirting. Not here, not yet.*

The man was impossible, irreverent, and totally perfect on so many levels it made her heart squeeze. After five years, she still hadn't gotten him out from under her skin.

"You look pale," Martin fussed. The elevator doors glided open and he put a hand on her elbow to usher her into the swank glass box. "And too skinny. Don't they feed you in Washington? Would you like breakfast on the veranda? I'll have Chef Condor make all your favorites!"

Everyone could see them inside the glass elevator. Bree took a deep breath and pasted on a bright smile, as if she were as carefree and lighthearted as any heir to a fortune could be. "That would be wonderful."

Her gaze skimmed the foyer, briefly noting that while everyone else in Martin's lineup had made haste to get back to work, one man still stood watching her.

Aidan.

She swallowed the lump that rose in her throat as their eyes met across the expanse. Silently, the doors closed but they were glass as well, so she kept smiling and dragged her attention from him to put it on her uncle. "I'd like to unpack first, then I'm all yours."

The elevator rose as her uncle heartily agreed. Be smart, she told herself again, digging deep into her willpower *not* to look at Aidan.

As Uncle Martin chatted away, she schooled her face into deep interest, but she snuck one tiny glance out the door just as the first floor slid out of sight.

Aidan was no longer staring at her.

He was gone.

THERE IS ALWAYS some madness in love...

Another saying her mother was fond of spouting. She'd say it almost whimsically, as if the madness of love was alluring, magical.

For Bree, love was the opposite... it was literally, well, maddening.

Uncle Martin deposited her in the Crystal Breeze suite on the top floor, with the most amazing views of the Gulf, even though Bree had asked for a smaller room near the pool. "Family comes first," he'd insisted, ushering her into the beautiful, upscale rooms that only his most important—and richest—clients could reserve. He'd left her to unpack, humming as he departed, Princess Gracie, his spoiled Chihuahua, in tow.

The suite was bigger than her apartment in DC, her single bag, already delivered by the bellhop, looking small and forlorn in the center of the main room. The warm woods and ivory furniture were the perfect complement to the backdrop of the shimmering blue waters outside. She kicked off her shoes and wandered to the glass patio doors, sliding them open and stepping onto the veranda.

The day was so clear, the morning sun bounced off the water, making it look like millions of diamonds floating on the surface. The private beach was mostly empty, the call of birds and an occasional *shishing* of palm leaves filling the air.

She'd left DC in a deep freeze.

Speaking of deep freezes… Drawing in a deep, salt-filled breath, she tried to shake off the aftereffects of seeing Aidan again. She'd spent the whole way here prepping herself, going over and over her assignment in order to stay detached.

How's that working for you?

Her legs felt shaky, her heart as well. Madness, that's what this was. How could she still feel so…infatuated…with a man she hadn't laid eyes on in two years?

Placing her hands on the railing, she considered throwing in the towel. Beatrice had sent her here, and Bree had known better than to accept the mission.

Bring him home, Beatrice had said. *Make him trust you again.*

Little did her boss realize what doing that would cost Bree.

But the words Beatrice *hadn't* said held just as much weight. *You owe me.*

Boy, did she. Two missions, two screwups. Mia's brush with violence in Monte Carlo hadn't technically been Bree's fault, but she still felt responsible since it had happened shortly after the brush pass they'd executed in the casino.

Cassandra's near death in Vienna, on the other hand, was entirely her fault. She'd been assigned to keep the SFI attorney safe and out of harm's way. Instead, Cassie still fought with her compromised immune system after being bitten by a bat infected with a fatal disease. If Bree hadn't gotten distracted, had stuck to Cassie like glue, it never would have happened.

Beatrice shouldn't have sent her in undercover. Talk about madness. The lawyer had no skills, no training in field operations, but that wasn't Bree's call. Beatrice had made the decision to let Cassie go undercover and Bree's only job had been to watch her back.

After that FUBAR, she'd turned in her resignation. She knew how it would go if she stayed. She'd once been a highly-esteemed CIA operative with a file full of commendations, and then she'd screwed up there too. First her mother's death, then Aidan, then...Russia.

That final, crucial mission the CIA had used her as a throwaway—an agent they considered expendable—and if it hadn't been for Aidan...

Cold snaked up her spine and she slammed the door on that fiasco. Nothing good would come from rehashing those memories yet again.

When Beatrice had shown up on her doorstep with a couple SFI team members, both former SEALs, and a noted psychologist, and gave Bree the choice of going to South Padre Island and completing an important mission, or sitting there with the psychologist and "working through" her issues, Bree had felt manipulated. Damned if she did, damned if she didn't.

No way she was embracing talk therapy, even if she respected and liked Dr. Emma Collins in every way possible. Bree's former teammates—Mick Ranger and Trace Hunter— had done a good job insisting Bree wasn't the only one to blame. They all shared the guilt and neither man held it against her.

A soft breeze picked up a strand of her hair and blew it across her face. While her guilt over Cassie hadn't waned, she appreciated the fact that Beatrice and the others had made an effort to convince her to let it go. To move on.

To recruit her husband—a former SEAL and CIA operative—to join the team.

It was the perfect fit, the Queen B insisted. Beatrice, head of Shadow Force International, had a well-oiled machine of ex-SEALs for certain tasks requiring specific skill sets: bodyguards, paramilitary missions, undercover work.

The latter missions had grown lately, and she'd been recruiting a few spies. Former ones, such as Bree, were a good match, but to have someone like Aidan? He was gold in the Queen's book.

But what would it cost Bree to win him over? To take him from her uncle—the only real family she had left in the world? Bree had been the one to send Aidan to Martin after her estranged husband left the Agency. He'd been "retired" just like she had, once they got him out of that Russian prison.

RED—*retired, extremely dangerous*. That's what they labeled her when they'd kicked her to the curb. Aidan had been given the same designation.

He'd saved her life over there, the least she could do when he got back on his feet after being tortured in that god-awful Russian prison was to help him get a job. Heading up the Gulf Breeze Spa & Resort security team seemed like the perfect gig. Uncle Martin had been desperate for someone to handle it and Aidan had needed to get out of DC and find a new home.

One far away from her.

Her watch blipped with an incoming call and she glanced at the number. Sighing, she went inside to get her cell and answer.

"Status update?" Beatrice asked as her way of greeting.

"I'm here."

"Have you made contact with our target?"

Eye contact. Did that count? "Yes."

"Good. You have three days. I'll expect you, with the package acquired, on Monday."

And if she failed? The resignation that had been rescinded would probably become a pink slip. "I won't let you down."

As she hung up, she felt the madness closing in. Aidan wouldn't even speak to her, how was she going to convince him to leave Texas and go back to DC to play spy again?

Bree tossed the phone on the bed, slid her shoes back on and headed for the door.

I have one job, and by God, I'm going to complete it if it kills me.

Knowing her husband, it just might.

TWO

W *in over people when necessary*

MARTIN DEMARCO TOOK SECURITY SERIOUSLY. Not only were his clients important and often followed by paparazzi, over eager fans, and stalkers, but Martin had once been an undercover agent for the CIA in Argentina. From what Aidan understood, the stint had been brief—less than a year—before the man reunited with his estranged family and took over part of their billion-dollar resort company's holdings. When his sister—Bree's mother—passed away from breast cancer, her share went to her daughter. Bree never wanted to run a company and insisted her uncle take full control.

Aidan took security seriously, too, and that was why, as he made his way down the steps to the lower veranda where Martin and Bree were having a late brunch, he planned to ignore the fact Bree was his wife. For today, for right now, as she sat in the sun throwing her head back with laughter at something her uncle said, she was a guest at the Gulf Breeze and would be afforded the same level and measures of personal security as any guest or member of his boss's family.

"That's your wife?" Joey, tagging along, kept his voice low as he descended the stairs with Aidan. "You never told me you were married."

"It's...complicated." The marriage was a sham, a mistake. At least, that's what Bree had told him. At Joey's questioning look, he added, "We're estranged."

"Why the hell would you be estranged from that?" He tilted his head toward the table, where Bree and all her beauty glowed as brightly as the sun.

Why indeed?

It's complicated didn't even begin to cover their relationship, and it certainly wasn't what he wanted. He'd fallen for her the first time he saw her in Vegas, and although she was the one mission he had utterly failed, he still felt the same heart-stopping desire for her as he did then.

Aidan ignored the question, engaging his *I don't give a fuck* face before halting on the landing of the veranda.

Joey stopped a foot back, also going into security guard mode—chest out, shoulders straight, no emotion on his face. He was a good kid who'd landed at the spa a few months after leaving the Air Force. Martin allowed Aidan to hire whomever he wanted, and Joey had been a shoe-in for his cyber security supervisor. During low season, he doubled as a bodyguard when other security staff took their vacations. Aidan never took one; Joey didn't either.

Princess Gracie, Martin's five pound Chihuahua, jumped off her cushioned bed near her master and ran to greet Aidan. He had a soft spot for the spoiled dog and couldn't resist her antics. For some reason, she seemed as nuts about him as she did Martin, and her owner often left her with Aidan when he had business to attend to. She ruled the roost and received as much pampering as any of the guests.

She barked once, dancing on her back feet and turning in a circle like a circus dog to show off for him. Then she scratched at his leg to get him to pick her up.

"Ah, there you are," Martin said, turning his attention to Aidan and Joey. "The eggs were getting cold so we started without you."

The veranda was only feet from the sandy beachfront, the lap of waves a soft backdrop to the impressive spread of food on the twelve-foot long table. Bree's eyes landed on him, sizing him up, and once again he felt that lack of oxygen, the squeeze of his lungs.

Shoving his reaction aside, he made a big deal out of scooping up the Chihuahua and tucking her under his arm as he scratched her chin. Her tail wagged a hundred miles an hour, and her bug eyes half-closed in blissful happiness.

"No problem." Aidan kept his attention on Martin. The man was more like a father than his employer. *You're part of the family*, Martin would often say. *I trust you like I would my own son.* The smell of bacon and waffles teased his nostrils, making his stomach growl. "I'm not hungry."

Bree snickered, easily spotting the lie as she always did. He was too far away for the sound of his growling stomach to have tipped her off, but she could see through his best acting job.

The temperature was climbing into the mid-seventies, a soft breeze dancing off the water. Pleasant conditions, and yet, Aidan felt a trickle of sweat slide under his collar.

"Nonsense," Martin said. "You work too hard, Aidan. Sit down, grab a plate, and join us."

Joey started to accept the invitation, and Aidan threw out a hand to stop him. No way did he want Joey in on the conversation. "Perimeter check," he ordered.

"But I thought Cortez was on—"

Aidan turned on him. "I want you to do it."

His tone brooked no argument and Joey dipped his head, turned on his heel, and marched off.

Strike two—not only did he have to make up his behavior to Megan, but now Joey as well. The day was off to a great start.

Placing Gracie on her cushion, he unbuttoned his suit coat and took a seat across from Bree. The butler, standing off to the side, stepped forward and poured him a cup of coffee.

"Thank you, Daniel," he said.

Without asking if he wanted any, Bree picked up a platter of bacon and handed it to him. Laying his napkin onto his lap, he accepted it and placed a heaping amount onto his plate. Next, she handed him a basket of biscuits, a container of honey, and slid the covered tray of scrambled eggs toward him, ignoring the one containing pancakes.

Honey instead of jam. Eggs instead of pancakes. Bacon instead of sausage. Three for three. In his book, that added up to her remembering. For some reason, that pleased him, but then he reminded himself she was a trained spy. She could probably do the same for the preferences of every person she'd ever worked with or investigated.

He made busy work of piling food onto his plate, even while he wondered why she was there, why was she visiting now, and if she recalled his preferences in other areas of their life, like the bedroom.

Martin beamed. For the past two years, he had encouraged Aidan to stay the course, reach out to Bree, and never give up. He knew his niece was strong-willed and stubborn, but he also believed she needed someone who could match her fiery passion and fierce loyalty.

"Tell us about your work," Martin said, turning to her. "Do you still love it?"

"Yes," she replied, and Aidan's bullshit meter went off. She was lying through her smile. "The company I work for is one of a kind, much like this beautiful place."

"That's wonderful." Martin was lying too. It wasn't that he wanted her to be unhappy, but if she loved her job, she had no reason to return to the DeMarco empire.

Aidan dug into his eggs, ignoring both of them, but listening carefully. Not just to their words, but what lay underneath.

Intelligence gathering. A hard habit to break.

"Well, I'm so glad you came home for the holidays. How long can you stay?" The big guy was a softy at heart, and even though he had no idea what had gone on between the two of them, he seemed to believe they could overcome it. That love conquered all, or some such bullshit. "Can you stay until New Year's, Bree? Tell me you can.!"

Always thinking positive. Always hoping.

But damn, his positive attitude had given Aidan hope too. He'd stayed in this job for the past two years with the pipe dream that Bree might "come home" as Martin called it. He was her only living relative now, and they'd become very close after her mother's death.

Plus, Aidan figured once Bree stopped running from her grief over her mother and decided to take up the reins of the family business, she'd need Martin's guidance. She'd come to the spa and Aidan would have a second chance to woo his wife.

Bree sat back in her chair and looked off at the Gulf. "I'm afraid I only have a few days. I have to be back in DC Monday."

Martin screwed up his face, sipped his coffee. A beeping

came from his watch, and he glanced at it, then rose. "Ah, I'm sorry, I forgot I have a call with an investor in a few minutes."

He tossed his napkin on the table and leaned over to kiss Bree's cheek. "No worries," she said. "We'll catch up later."

"I'll find you as soon as I'm free." He grinned at Aidan. "In the meantime, Aidan, stay with her and make sure all her needs are met, won't you?"

His mouth was full of biscuit and all he could do was nod.

"I'll have Megan get you in for a massage and hot-stone treatment," Martin said to Bree. "I know how much you love them."

Bree flashed her dazzling smile at the man and Aidan was mesmerized. He quit chewing to just stare. "Fabulous," she said. "All I want to do is relax and forget the outside world."

Princess Gracie hopped off her cushion and followed Martin. At the entrance, he glanced back and Bree waved, as if everything was fine. Great even.

Once he disappeared inside, the smile fell off her face as she turned her focus on Aidan. She dismissed Daniel, then sat in silence, staring at Aidan as if waiting for something.

He swallowed and put down his fork. From the look on her face, it was time to put on his boxing gloves. He sat back in his chair, mimicking her posture and stare. It was a challenge, a game. Whoever spoke first lost.

He'd be damned if it was going to be him.

"Well?" she finally inquired. "Aren't you going to ask what I'm doing here?"

The question of the hour, but there was one thing he wanted to know even more. "Are you okay, Bree?"

The challenge in her features softened. Her gaze darted to the water, back to him. "No," she admitted, and he could see the truth in her eyes. "But I will be. I just need..."

He waited for her to finish. She toyed with a napkin instead. "Need what?" he asked softly.

He assumed she would say "a divorce," so he was surprised —and then not—when she said, "I have a job."

Didn't that say it all? For her, nothing mattered except that. Not him, not her family fortune, not even Martin who so desperately wanted to share his life with her.

She wasn't there to see her uncle or try and work things out with Aidan. He had to admit, he felt slightly relieved she hadn't brought up the divorce papers. But he also suddenly felt angry, exasperated. She was on a *job*, a mission, an operation. Who did she work for these days? Not the CIA, not British Intelligence, but who?

He suppressed his anger, sipped his coffee, and schooled his face. This was the last thing he wanted to talk about, and she probably wouldn't tell him anyway because it was top secret. But the only way he could pierce that armor she had so tightly wrapped around her, to find common ground to meet on, was to be supportive. "You're safe here. Tell me what's going on and I'll see if I can help."

Obtaining 'of value' intelligence

AIDAN WANTED TO HELP HER? She almost laughed out loud. He wouldn't when he found out what she was about to ask him to do, but of course, without even knowing what she needed, he was offering to help. She sighed. He was such a damn nice guy. Dangerous, cunning, and calculating, sure. He knew who his enemies were and kept them far from him. If you were friend or family, however, he would do anything for you. He would even lay down his life to save yours. She knew that first hand.

He was always trying to help her, protect her, and she'd been a lousy wife and partner. He deserved much, much better than she could ever be.

She'd done her best to make it up to him, but she didn't know how, outside of pulling the strings to get him this cushy job. She was a different creature than he was, had learned to be completely independent. After her mother died, she'd forgotten how to love.

She wanted to love him, and let him love her, but every time she considered it, her heart jammed on the brakes. Love hurt, and she wasn't sure she could ever fully commit to anyone because the fear of losing them would shadow everything.

Yes, she loved Uncle Martin. He had become both father and mother to her through the years, and she owed him a great deal for all he'd done to keep the family business together while she struggled to find a purpose for her life.

Respecting her silence, Aidan stood and went to get the coffee carafe. He refilled their cups, giving her time to choose her words.

Trained in the world of spycraft, she was an expert at manipulating people, crafting her words to influence them to do what she wanted. She knew how to exploit weaknesses and turn assets to her way of thinking.

The one person she had never been able to do that with now resumed his seat across from her at the table. "I've never known you to be at a loss for words," Aidan said. "Must be serious. Pretty sweet ride you drove in here. New boyfriend?"

Four sentences loaded with all kinds of innuendo. Sparring came so naturally to them, he was using it to help her relax. He knew she'd never cheat on him, even if they were estranged.

"You think I need one in order to drive a Maserati? That I might not just pick it out for myself?"

A grin shone in his eyes even though his lips did no more than quirk. "You're not exactly a car aficionado. You didn't even have a driver's license until you went to work for the Agency."

A dig at her childhood, filled with chauffeurs and appointed drivers. "Maybe I've acquired a taste for flashy six cylinders."

"So, it's a company car. Who're you working for?"

Without her even trying to lead him to the topic, he'd segued right into it. "That's actually what I want to talk to you about. My employer."

For a split second, he looked relieved—probably because she hadn't brought up the divorce they never seemed to get around to—and then the relief morphed into curiosity. "Are you in trouble?"

Assuming the worst. She supposed she deserved that. "No. Even if I were, I would never lead my trouble to Uncle Martin. I'm not in any—well, not exactly. My last assignment didn't go the way it should have, and now I'm trying to make up for it, you might say."

A long moment of scrutiny. "Go on."

She was about to when Aidan's second-in-command appeared, slightly out of breath. He was young and cute, in that nerdy computer guy sort of way. He had muscles under his suit, but was wearing a Minecraft tie.

"Sorry to interrupt," he said to her before hastily turning his attention to Aidan. "We've got a problem, boss. One of our Alphas just arrived and has an issue with his room. He's giving Megan and Candace a lot of grief, demanding to see Mr. DeMarco, but he's on that conference call and ordered us not to interrupt him."

Aidan immediately rose and buttoned his jacket. "I'll be

right there," he said to the guy. To her, "Excuse me. I need to handle this."

He was going to handle it? The head of security? Pushing to her feet, Bree combed her fingers through her tangled hair and headed for the entrance. "I'll take care of it."

He fell into step beside her as she took the steps to the wide sidewalk. "What do you think you're going to do? This guy probably reserved the Crystal Breeze room and now you're in it. You better let me talk to him. I know him."

"I know how to talk to a guest and convince them to take a different room."

"He's an Alpha. He won't want a different room."

They made it to the French glass doors and Aidan opened one for her. As she passed through, she lowered her voice. "Fifty bucks says I can get him to accept a different room and be happy to do it."

He touched her lower back as they swept into the atrium. "You're on."

Across the way, she spotted the man leaning on the front desk arguing with Megan. Bree scanned him from the back. Medium height, dark hair, expensive suit and shoes. Beside his leg sat a single suitcase. A briefcase was slung over his shoulder.

His voice rose and fell, his French accent melodic even though he was upset. Candace shot a glance over the desk, catching Bree's eye. *Help* was clearly telegraphed.

Joey fell into step with her and Aidan. "Megan is a master at handling guests," he murmured, "but this guy won't be deterred."

"Name?" Bree asked.

"Etienne Chardy."

Bree winked at Candace and Megan to let the young women know she'd deal with the situation and to relax.

Candace gave her a relieved smile. Megan still looked flustered —upset that Martin's niece had to step in, Bree assumed.

"Mr. Chardy." As the man turned to see who was calling his name, Bree stuck out her hand and turned on her megawatt smile. In the field, she often had to use her beauty and personality to distract or divert her target. In the spa business, the same tactics worked on upset clients. "I'm so sorry for the inconvenience."

The man's dark eyes scanned her and softened at her smile. His skin was burnished by the sun, his lower face covered with a close cut beard. He hesitated only a moment before accepting her handshake. "I don't believe I've had the pleasure."

"I'm Martin's niece, Abreena. Call me Bree. He's tied up with a business matter at the moment, and sends his apologies. He'll catch up with you later. In the meantime, I'm here to help."

The man's gaze roamed over her, lingering on her breasts. "I didn't realize Martin had a niece, and such a beautiful one at that."

She kept her smile in place, even though she imagined telling him her eyes were on her face, not her chest. "I understand you reserved one of the penthouse suites?"

Chardy glanced at Aidan, gave him a nod of acknowledgment, then his attention bounced over to Candace and Megan. "I reserved the Crystal Breeze two months ago, and now I'm told I can't have it. I always reserve that suite. I'm supposed to have it for the whole week."

There was something in the way he acknowledged Aidan, or perhaps it was his profile, that triggered the faintest memory in the back of her mind. It was so fleeting she couldn't make sense of it.

No time to figure it out now. "Yes, of course. Unfortunately, there's a bit of a plumbing problem." She scrunched up her nose as if it were disgusting and it was better she didn't go into details. "I'm terribly sorry, but believe me, you do *not* want to be in that suite right now."

She waved a hand under her nose, emphasizing the fact the issue was ugly...or *smelly* in this case. "We have someone working on it, of course, but things are really *backed up.*" *If you get my drift.* "I'm told it's going to be a couple days before the suite is ready, but I can move you in there as soon as the problem is resolved." She leaned in close and lowered her voice. "I want to make sure it's absolutely aired out before we put you in there."

She straightened and hit him with her megawatt smile again. "What is it about that room that you love the most? I bet it's the view, isn't it?"

Before he could answer, she took his arm, nodded at Candace, and went into her sales pitch. "We have an amazing set of rooms right underneath it with the same exact view, and they're connected. The two combined are the same size as the suite. Let me show you that combo and see if it will meet your needs. For your inconvenience, we'll take ten percent off your final bill" —she nodded at Megan to be sure the assistant took care of it— "and throw in your choice of packages for the spa."

She could see the calculations going on in his brain. Two rooms versus one, a discount, and the same view. What was there to think about?

Candace and Megan both nodded, letting Bree know the connecting rooms were open and the package would be handled. Both were flushed and seemed to be holding a collective breath.

Joey was off to the side, hiding a smile. Aidan stood behind her, but she could feel tension radiating off him as though she were violating some secret code. Either he was annoyed at

Chardy's ogling, or pissed because he knew this was going to cost him fifty bucks.

Calculations over, Chardy smiled. "Very well, I suppose I could at least have a look."

Score. "You're going to love them," she gushed, pulling him toward the elevators. "I often prefer to stay in them when I visit, and use one solely for business,"—she glanced at his briefcase—"reserving the other for relaxation only. Helps me separate the two and reminds me not to work so much."

When he reached back to grab his luggage, Aidan stepped in. "I've got it, sir."

Chardy allowed him to take the suitcase as they walked. "Is she telling the truth? Will I be wowed by this arrangement?"

Again, that familiarity with Aidan. "Guess there's only one way to find out," he answered.

"It's up to my standards for security?"

Aidan nodded. "Just swept it this morning. It's clean."

Clean? Of what, listening devices? Cameras? Who was this guy? She covertly scanned his face again. That, combined with his voice, kept making her brain fire in the memory department, but she couldn't for the life of her place him.

He caught her eyes and gave her a flirty smile, as though letting her know he knew she was snowing him. "Martin must be pleased you're here, helping him with the business."

"He's taught me everything I know."

Chardy's eyes darkened slightly and he nodded. "I'm sure he has, Abreena."

The way he said her name made that memory bell go off yet again. He now looked at her as though he knew her. The familiarity in his voice was the same as he'd used on Aidan.

She would have to grill Aidan once they were alone. She punched the button and the doors immediately opened. As the three of them got in, Joey sent her a thumbs-up from the desk,

Candace was grinning, and Bree glanced at Aidan behind Chardy's back and waggled her eyebrows. His face was stone, giving her nothing in return.

Yup, he was pissed about the money. He should've known better than to bet against her.

Before the doors shut, she made a motion to Megan, signaling to send up champagne. The woman nodded quickly and began typing on her computer to forward the order to the kitchen.

On the third floor, Bree continued to play hostess, giving Chardy the tour of both rooms and talking them up. Aidan deposited the man's suitcase near the closet of the first room and took up residence in the hallway.

In her line of work, she had to have a good memory for faces and names, yet as she showed him the view from the patio doors and led him onto the enclosed veranda overlooking the beach, she couldn't place him.

Maybe she had come across him at some other time, perhaps even here at the hotel. Some of their guests were repeats coming back year after year. He might be one of those, and from the looks of it, he definitely planned to work along with enjoying the hotel's amenities. He kept his briefcase, even outside as he placed his hands on the railing and took a deep breath of the salt air.

"What do you think?" she asked. "Will this work for you until we can move you upstairs?"

He nodded, looking at the water before shifting his dark eyes to her. His lashes were thick and dark as well, making him appear to have eyeliner on. "I'll try it for tonight and let you know in the morning."

There was something in those eyes, something in the smile he gave her. An invitation mixed with a little challenge. He liked her, but wasn't about to let her off the hook easily.

"I can't ask for anything else," she replied sweetly. "I appreciate your flexibility, and I promise, as soon as the plumbing upstairs is fixed and the room is up to our exceptional standards, we'll get you moved in."

The champagne arrived, one of the busboys bringing it in to the round table near the patio door. "Thank you, Miguel," she said, stepping inside. The young man nodded and left, Chardy following on her heels.

"Compliments of the house," she said. "Please let me know if there's anything else I can help you with."

She was about to walk away when he said, "You could stay and have a glass with me."

She tried to appear surprised and flattered, but the warning bell in her head grew louder. She needed to talk to Aidan, needed to figure out why. She couldn't just beg off and say she had to get back to work. She didn't technically work here, and she needed to finish her conversation with her husband. "That's very generous of you, but I'm afraid I can't."

No meant no, except to some men, including the one in front of her. "It would make me like this arrangement better."

Flirting and bribing her at the same time. He was smooth. She could claim an appointment, a previous engagement, but that would only give him an opening to ask her to come back later. She had to nip this in the bud without pissing him off.

Luckily, she had just the thing to do that. She pretended to be slightly remorseful as she pulled the long chain from around her neck, allowing the platinum band on the end to swing in the air. Smiling sweetly, she said, "I'm afraid my husband wouldn't like it if I did that."

Before he could say anything else, she left the room and found Aidan in the hallway, pure annoyance on his face.

THREE

The first rule of spying: don't get found out

BREE HAD NEVER ANSWERED his question. He'd been fishing when he asked about the car and boyfriend, and she'd known it. No doubt she wanted to make him squirm, wondering who she was spending time with these days.

More to the point, he didn't like being used as an excuse to shut down a philanderer, when she didn't openly recognize their marriage any other time.

She kept pace with him as they left Chardy's room and entered the elevator, neither saying anything until the doors shut.

He reached for the first floor button; she stayed his hand. "We're going up," she said. She hit the penthouse and swiped her keycard and started their ascent. "We need to finish our earlier conversation."

Exactly what he wanted, but he found himself being disagreeable anyway. "I have to work."

She canted her body to lean against the wall, crossing her arms over her chest. "Why is Mr. Chardy so concerned with security? Why is he worried about bugs?"

Schooling his features and forcing his shoulders to relax, he met her gaze. "Why are you wearing your wedding band around your neck?"

The corners of her eyes narrowed slightly at his attempt at diversion. "We're married, aren't we? Who is he?"

Diversion never worked with her. She'd always been skilled at carrying on multiple conversations at the same time. Unfortunately, he needed to get her off Chardy's track or she'd blow everything. "Funny, you don't act like a married woman."

Her eyes narrowed even more. "You realize trying to rile me up about our relationship to keep me from inquiring about our new guest only makes me want to know more about him?"

The elevator stopped at her penthouse, the doors opening directly into the gleaming foyer. He motioned for her to go ahead of him, but she shook her head. "You first."

She read his mind, figuring out his plan to go down to the main floor the moment she exited.

Damn, even after two years of hardly seeing her, she still knew him too well. Probably because she was the one who'd trained him at Camp Swampy.

His time there had been easy in comparison to SEAL training, but still a contrasting kind of world. He'd been a different man, and she'd been a ruthless trainer. At the height of her career with the Agency, she'd managed to keep their impromptu wedding a secret, their marriage unknown even to the CIA for a while, and when he'd shown up in her escape and evasion class, she never so much as blinked.

Like now, as she held the doors open, waiting for him to move first.

The two of them were like fire and ice, Aidan just wasn't sure who would survive in the end. They'd both been down and out when they met in Vegas. While she denied it, and would until her deathbed, he knew they'd saved each other. And again in Russia. `

He entered the penthouse, going to the large kitchen area. He needed caffeine. His head hurt, still hung over from the morning's nightmare, lack of sleep, and the surprise of seeing Bree, all combined to make his muscles twitch. He heard her kick off her shoes behind him and flop down on the large couch. Once the high-end coffee maker was brewing, he turned to face her, leaning against the counter and crossing his feet at his ankles.

Play it cool. She's already suspicious, and you can't have her looking into Chardy's background. "Etienne Chardy is a Canadian financier who visits the spa every six months or so. He deals in high-tech stocks and international investments." *Among other things you don't need to know about.* "His concerns regarding his room relate to cyber security and keeping his clients' personal investment information from getting hacked. That's all."

She studied him for a long moment, the smell of premium roasted coffee filling the air between them. "Do you really need to get back to work right away?"

He felt his lungs release the air they were holding. Had he really convinced her to drop her interest in the man? "Believe it or not, even when things are slow, I have plenty to do. Your uncle has given me more responsibilities than just security, and the off season is when we look at upgrades and revamping certain systems to work more effectively."

She stretched out her long legs, setting her feet on the

coffee table. Running her fingers through her hair, she leaned her head back on the cushion and let out a deep sigh. "Okay, is there a time when you're off the clock and we can talk?"

Cooperation? Consideration? She again surprised him.

She was so damn beautiful, the red dress flowing like water over her curves. He remembered them well and dreamed about them—a different form of PTSD. The memory of her under him, on top of him, beside him, was its own brand of torture, one he was more than willing to repeat.

Those legs, those hips, those very generous breasts... every part of her, right up to her full lips and long hair made his cock twitch. His hands tingled with the need to touch her.

And that was another reason he had to get the hell out of here, put distance between them, because if he didn't...

Clearing his throat and spinning around, he tried to shutdown thoughts of her, naked, in his bed, in a shower, in the backseat of his car. His cock grew hard, despite his best efforts, and would be an obvious giveaway about what was flooding his mind, so he made himself busy finding two mugs, even though he had no intention of staying around for a drink now.

Focusing on the bland subject of coffee, keeping his attention glued to the process of pouring it and setting the carafe back on the burner, he forced himself to breathe deeply and blank out everything else. When he once more had his body under control, the ache for her shut behind a door and his mind locked in on his escape, he casually took one and handed it to her. She accepted, blowing on the liquid to cool it before taking a sip.

"I'm officially off the clock at six." He was generally always on call, but he was allowed to adjust as needed this time of year. "I'll text you and we can meet up for a drink or something."

"If Chardy reserved this penthouse, does that mean you've swept it for bugs and cameras?"

She was back to that. "Joey and I are religious about scrubbing the rooms between guests. There are more than a few spies who come through here, as you well know, and there's always the chance paparazzi or a private investigator might try to garner personal information by staying in a room and leaving something like that behind."

"Of course. Any spies I might know come through recently?"

God, she was too nosy for her own good. "I have no idea how many spies you know, and most that stay here seek total anonymity, so I couldn't share that information even if I had it."

She smiled smugly. "This place technically belongs to me— I *am* the heir to the DeMarco fortune and all its assets. The guest list isn't confidential to me."

"Pretty sure it is unless you've given up your spying ways to come home and run the place."

She rolled her eyes. "You don't want me doing that."

"No argument there."

A narrowing of her eyes again suggested she would kick him if he were closer. "You owe me fifty bucks."

Sighing, but relieved she was dropping the Chardy thing, he reached into his back pocket, found a fifty, and tossed it at her. "You can use it to buy me dinner tonight."

Leaving his coffee untouched, he sauntered to the foyer. "The Winter Lights Hop open house is tomorrow night. You might see if Candace and Megan can use help with last minute details, Miss Owner."

"What is that?"

"A new thing the Chamber of Commerce is doing to bring shoppers to the island for the holidays. Businesses decorate and offer a prize package of their goods or services and people hop up and down the island to enter the giveaways and finish their holiday shopping."

"That's a great idea."

He'd almost made his escape, convinced he'd diffused the issue about Chardy and put her mind on other things. He climbed into the elevator, and as he pushed the button to take him to the main floor, she waved at him. "Chardy looks familiar to me. I don't know who he is, but I'll find out."

He smiled reluctantly, feeling that old flame of desire flare again. That nosiness was damning, and he was going to have keep her away from Chardy, no matter what it took, or risk her screwing up his operation.

And heaven be damned, he was actually looking forward to the challenge.

GHOST SURVEILLANCE

As soon Aidan left, Bree pulled out her phone and did a search on Etienne Chardy.

She came up blank. There were plenty with the last name, even two with the first, but none fit the man staying below her. Was he using his real name? It wouldn't be the first time someone reserved a room under a false name. Plenty of rich and famous came here to get away from their hectic, public lives.

Maybe that was why he looked familiar. He was someone in the public eye she'd seen or read about.

A niggling feeling in her belly argued there was more to it. She wasn't sure why she cared, outside of the fact Aidan had gone to great lengths to pretend their guest was nobody to worry about. That very fact screamed at her. While Aidan's poker face was one of the best she'd ever seen, she knew him on a level most didn't. Estranged or not, she'd always been able to tell when he was hedging or outright lying.

In training, and in the field, no one had ever been able to spot his tells—the barely there signs he wasn't being forthright and honest—except her.

He was an ace at subterfuge. One of the best she'd ever trained, maybe even as good as she was. Yet, she could tell, even after being away from him for the past two years, that he was hiding something.

She'd seen it flicker in in his eyes before he could stamp it out, sense it in the tension between his shoulders, even though he'd tried to appear relaxed. If Mr. Chardy was nothing more than what Aidan claimed, why had he seemed determined to keep her in the dark about him?

Sipping her coffee, she continued to dig, accessing social media, professional sites, and then, when she still couldn't find anything on the financier, she called Rory at SFI headquarters.

"My favorite goddess," he greeted her. "What can I do for you, Hathor?"

A retired spook who'd been one of the best assassins the CIA ever had, Rory was a legend in her book. He was listed by the Agency now as RED like her and Aidan but knew neither of them could hold a candle to the man. "I need information on a guest staying here." She gave him the man's—fake?— name and what little she knew about him. "I did several searches across the Internet and came up with zilch."

"Something about him tickling your fancy?"

"It's weak, but he seems vaguely familiar. I get an itch every time he talks to me. It's like he knows me, but I don't know him, and I think this name and identity are totally bogus."

"Does that matter? I don't believe your assignment involves investigating guests, does it?"

He knew it didn't. "I'm well aware of what my assignment entails but there's something off and I want to know what it is. Will you humor me?"

She heard typing in the background. "Never ignore the itch, I say. I'll do some digging and get back to you if I find anything."

"Can you keep this on the down-low for now?" The last thing she wanted was Beatrice to find out she was looking for trouble rather than making amends with her husband.

"No guarantees, Hathor, but for you? I'll do what I can. You know the Queen B has ESP, right?"

It did seem that way. "I'm going to complete my assignment and make her a very happy woman. While I'm doing that, I might sniff out a bad guy. No harm in that, is there?"

More typing. "Does seem suspicious the guy has nothing on the net. Talk soon."

The connection ended and she tossed her phone on the couch next to her. Tonight she would recruit Aidan over dinner and drinks. She'd have to be on her best behavior and not rub it in about the fifty dollars and her always being right. In other words, wine him and dine him, and get him to agree to come back to DC and work for her boss.

Piece of cake.

It was the farthest thing from that, but she had to psych herself up. She'd had much harder assignments in the past.

She unpacked her meager belongings, finished her coffee, and met up with Martin a little while later. He was very excited about the new investor—a brother and sister team in Paris who wanted to bring the DeMarco brand to Europe.

"We'll start with one location on the Avenue Montaigne, along with our line of Rejuve spa lotions at all the major retail chains throughout France. I'm flying there Monday to meet with them and their board of directors." He clapped his hands together, Princess Gracie dancing at his feet as if the excitement were for her. "Can you stay and run things until I get back?"

"Stay?"

"Don't look so horrified. It will only be a few days, and Aidan told me you handled Etienne Chardy like an old pro. You're a natural."

"Why did you give me his suite when he had it booked already?"

Martin waved a hand in the air. "Family comes first. Don't worry. If he's still pissed, I'll make it up to him. Now, tell me you'll stay and take care of *this* family"—he pointed to the dog and then the building—"while I'm away. I need you here."

The DeMarco business was her grandparents' legacy with locations in all of the top US cities. The Rejuve line of lotions, massage oils, and supplements capitalized on their elite clientele's desire for endless youth and pampering. Bree still used the line to this day that her mother had developed when she was in her teens.

But run this place? Even for such a short time? God only knew the damage she might do. "I don't know, Uncle Martin."

Yes, she had training in the basics of how things worked having spent the majority of her youth growing up here. But she was no Martin DeMarco.

"You can't take a few extra days from your job to help me out?" He looked up at the ceiling as if searching Heaven for her mother. "Your daughter is going to give me a heart attack, Mary Rachel. She won't even help her poor uncle out."

Bree rolled her eyes and playfully pinched his arm. "Stop that. You're doing a great job and don't need me."

He ran things from South Padre Island because it had been the founding spa her grandparents had built, his own childhood memories dear to him as well. Plus, he loved the weather. He made regular trips to the other locations, making sure each lived up to the DeMarco standard, but always lived here.

She'd never been cut out for running one of the sites, much less the entire company, and thanked God every day her uncle had both a love for the business and a head for it.

He scooped up Princess Gracie and scratched under her chin as they walked toward the dining room. "While you're in charge, it'll give you and Aidan time to work things out."

There was no working anything out, but she loved him for being as much of a romantic as her mother had been. "Why haven't you ever married?" she asked.

"No changing the subject." He waggled a finger at her, his face stern. "You came down here to see Aidan, not your dear old uncle, and I insist you give that husband of yours another chance. You both deserve happiness and I can see the sparks fly every time the two of you are together."

She damn well *was* going to change it. "Your holiday decorations aren't up to par for this weekend. This is an elite boutique spa and hotel. You don't even have the tree up in the lobby." In her youth, there'd always been a giant tree in the center of the check-in area, drawing attention to the amazing view of the Gulf. "No lights even in the atrium? It's a disgrace."

He grinned broadly. "The tree and decorations are in the storage room. Have Miguel and Aidan help you get them out."

"You want me to put it up?"

"It was always your mother's favorite thing to do at the holidays."

He didn't have to remind her. A sense of coming full-circle, putting up the tree and decorating it herself, washed over her. "Fine, but I'm also calling in some help to get this place ready for tomorrow night."

He came to a stop, facing her. His grin fell, but his eyes still danced. "How much is that going to cost me?"

"Hey, you're getting my services for free, so don't complain."

"You're staying?"

"I make no promises." She lifted her chin. "My boss has given me orders to return on Monday. I'll do what I can to get an extension"—she was probably going to need it—"but I may not have a choice."

"I can speak to your boss if you'd like."

Oh *hell* no. "I'm thirty-two years old. I don't need you running interference for me."

They reached the dining area. Through the beautiful French doors, she saw Etienne Chardy eating a salad.

"You're not taking Princess Gracie in there, are you?" she asked her uncle.

"Why not?"

She gave him a shocked look. "Can you say health code violation?"

It was his turn to roll his eyes. "Do you see the health inspector here?"

"What if one of the guests report you?"

"And risk shutting this place down? Pul-*lleazzz*. Half of them bring their dogs, and those spoiled pooches accompany them to the dining room, down to the beach, everywhere!"

Sometimes he could be overly dramatic. She took the Chihuahua from his arms, enjoying a royal lick from the little girl. "I'll get Gracie some lunch. You speak to Mr. Chardy and make sure he's truly okay with the room change. If not, I'll pretend the plumbing is fixed and I'll move down here by the infinity pool."

"Chardy will be fine. Don't worry about it. We have more catching up to do. I want to hear all about your job."

His grin was teasing. She suspected he knew she couldn't talk about it, but liked to tease her endlessly. "I have a giant Christmas tree to put up and decorate. After lunch, you can help me."

"I have the feeling you're avoiding me."

"I never would, but you know I can't tell you details about what I do or who I work for."

He made an exasperated face. "You're working for the Agency again, aren't you? I knew it."

Martin had been quite a few things in his day, including an undercover operative for the CIA for a brief period. He'd been the first she told when they recruited her while she was still in college. She'd never dreamed of working for them, but after gleaning information about one of her teachers for them, in conjunction with MI5, the spying gig had been in her blood.

"They kicked me out, why would they hire me back?" It still irritated her. "More importantly, why would I ever want them to?"

He nodded, seemingly appeased. "Why is it a secret, then? Is it the NSA? The Feds?"

"None of the above. The group I work for is top notch, very close knit." In fact, Beatrice referred to Shadow Force as a family, and it kind of was. An extraordinarily trained one specializing in highly secret paramilitary and undercover oper-ations, but still, everyone was close. That was why her last failed mission ate at her so much. They'd almost lost Cassan-dra. "Everyone there has my back."

"I worry about you, you know."

She kissed his cheek and patted his arm. "There's no need to. I'm fine."

Once he was inside the dining room chatting with Chardy, she withdrew her phone and pretended to text. She managed to get several shots of Chardy and sent them to Rory. Maybe facial recognition could pick up the man's identity.

"What are you doing?"

Startled, she whirled to find Aidan behind her. Princess Gracie gave a little bark and wagged her tail, delighted to see him and practically launching herself from Bree's hold. "Oh my gosh, where did you come from?"

He gave her the stink eye. "Were you just taking pictures of one of our guests?"

Busted. Pulse tripping over itself, she pocketed the phone and tried to school her expression. He was so close she could feel the heat coming off his body. "I was taking one of my uncle enjoying himself at lunch. Is that okay with you?"

His intense focus shifted to Chardy, back to her. She could see the wheels spinning in his head. Why did he care if she was?

Unless there was something going on with that guest he wasn't admitting to. Bingo.

She didn't give him time to answer her question or probe for proof on her phone. "Uncle Martin said you and Miguel could help me get the Christmas tree out of storage. We need to get this place shaped up for the Winter Lights Hop. First, I have to feed Princess Gracie, so I'll meet you two in the lounge across from the receptionist desk in twenty minutes."

"Christmas tree?" He sounded incredulous.

"Yes," she said, heading down the hallway. "And don't forget the boxes of decorations. There should be five or six of them," she called over her shoulder.

Before she turned the corner, she glanced back. Aidan was still standing there, as unmoving as the shadows, staring after her.

In the next twenty minutes, she fed the dog, had Megan call the local florist, and managed to resist bugging Chardy's room. Aidan would catch her on camera, no doubt. Surely he had them in all the hallways, the elevators, and stairs. She could sneak off her balcony and try slipping down a floor to Chardy's, but that was better done under the cover of night and Aidan no doubt had alarms on all the entrances and exits.

When she finally made it to the lobby, she saw the tree was already up. Miguel was opening the decorations and Candace had wandered over to help.

She glanced around, but there was no Aidan. Had he intentionally slipped away so he wouldn't have to do this?

"The florist will be here shortly with the fresh wreath and pine boughs you ordered," Megan said as she hustled by. "I'll help as soon as I make sure Reba you-know-who gets her power shake."

Bree set Princess Gracie down who immediately began sniffing at the base of the tree. "Is Loretta still running the island florist?" she asked Candace.

Candace pulled out a roll of wide silver ribbon. "Yep! No slowing her down. She's just like your uncle and loves running her own business. Megan caught her right before she was leaving to make deliveries—I guess a lot of the shops are sprucing up for the hop too. She's got two buckets of extra pine and spruce boughs she said would be perfect for the fireplace mantel, and the wreath is one from her own shop's door. She said it would look better on our front desk."

Loretta had been a friend of Bree's mother. "She's still working full-time then?"

Candace nodded. "She lives for that place. Her daughter bought the building next door and has an interior design business in it. She keeps an eye on Loretta and they share clientele. Usually, it's just Tom making deliveries, but Loretta said they have so many today, she's doing a few herself."

Bree put Miguel on light duty and had Candace lay out all

of the ribbons on the nearby couches. Outside, a fine drizzle began, and several people who'd been walking the beach came hustling in. Candace grabbed towels from the massage rooms, Bree turned on the fireplace, and the guests offered to help with the decorating. Bree began unpacking the boxes of ornaments.

Over the speakers, Christmas music took the place of piano tunes, and Joey came walking in a minute later, asking her if that was okay. Everyone said yes, and Bree had him help Miguel with the lights.

A little while later, Condor, the chef, brought a tray of frosted sugar cookies and cups of hot cocoa. Bree invited the man to join them, and he did, telling stories about Christmas in his hometown in Nigeria and sneaking tiny pieces of sugar cookie to the dog.

Loretta showed up with the greens, wreath, and more ribbon. She also gave a beautiful holiday arrangement to Megan, who blushed when she read the card. Candace oohed and aahed over it, and Megan said under her breath, "They're from Aidan!"

Both women giggled together, their backs to Bree, but she heard them. Candace snuck a glance at her, and Bree pretended to be busy hugging Loretta.

Loretta accepted a cookie and a cup of cocoa and praised them on the decorations they already had up. "Your mama always loved the silver bells theme," she said. Her hair was long and gray, but beautiful. "She'd be so proud to see you carrying on her tradition."

Bree smiled, watching Candace and Miguel hang frosted blue and silver ornaments. Joey hustled in with a stepladder so they could reach the upper sections of the eleven foot tree.

"I miss her every day," Bree said quietly, forgetting the sick feeling Megan's flowers evoked in her.

Loretta squeezed her arm. "It's so good to have you back. Are you staying for good this time?"

I wish I could. "A visit is all I can manage right now."

Loretta took another sip of her cocoa and nodded. "I'm sure Martin is thrilled. He's such a good guy." She patted Princess Gracie, now lying on the couch supervising the activities and scanning the floor in case any crumbs might appear. "I better get to work on the fireplace mantle. Linda is minding the store, but it's a busy weekend, so I can't be gone long."

"How is Linda?"

"She's doing great, owns her own business now. I'm so blessed she came back to the island and bought the place next to mine. I get to see her every day, and we help each other out. If you have time, you should stop over and say hi. I know she'd be thrilled to see you."

Bree had many memories of playing in the sand with Linda. How different each of their lives had become. "I'm happy for both of you, and if I can, I'll run by so I can see her and her new business."

People were laughing and joking, a few of them humming and singing along with the Christmas carols. It had been such a long time since Bree had been around friends and family at the holidays, she'd forgotten how satisfying it could be.

She was handing Joey the star for the top of the tree when her phone buzzed. Caller ID said Tech Support. She walked away from the festivities to the large glass doors looking out onto the sand and water. Storm clouds hovered and rain drenched the outdoor patios. "Did you get a hit?"

Rory's voice was tentative. "Sort of."

"What does that mean?"

He chuckled. "Can you give me any video of this guy? Walking, moving around, so I can retrieve some body biomarkers?"

Bree glanced over her shoulder. Everyone was focused on the tree and socializing with each other. She felt a pang of melancholy hit her solar plexus—*Mom really would love seeing this,* she thought. "I can try, why?"

"The pictures you sent were mostly in profile. He has a couple markers that match one of the people in our database, but it's not enough to say for sure. Video would be better, or at least more straight-on headshots. There's something odd about this."

You're telling me. She turned and looked out at the waves on the water. "Who's the match in the database?"

"I'd rather not say until I know for sure we have absolute proof. The matches were in the chin and earlobe, but nothing else. I want at least ten that match. When I have only two, it could be an anomaly."

Earlobes were very individual. She understood Rory's need for absolute proof, yet her gut told her she was onto something. "Earlobes don't lie, Rory. Who's the match?"

He sighed, but before he could reply, she felt a wall of heat against her back.

"I found another box of ornaments."

She jumped so hard, she dropped her phone. It went spinning across the tile floor, bouncing into the French door. Hand on chest, Bree sore softly. "Jesus, Aidan. Will you stop sneaking up on me?"

He tilted his head slightly, eyeing the phone on the floor before meeting her eyes again. "Why are you so jumpy?"

She hustled over to pick up the phone. "Sorry about that," she said to Rory. Her eyes fell on the box in Aidan's hand and her breath caught. She pointed at it. "Where did you find that?"

He shrugged nonchalantly, but she could see the wheels spinning again as he tried to figure out who she was speaking to.

"On a shelf in the back. Has your name on it but wasn't sure if you wanted it or not."

Her heart plunged, seeing her mother's handwriting, her name in the beautiful script. "I, uh…"

The word stuck in her throat, a hard lump.

"Hathor?" Rory's voice was concerned. "Everything okay?"

Tucking the phone between her ear and shoulder and grabbing the box out of Aidan's hand, she fought the tears burning in her eyes as she fled the lounge area and ran for the elevators. "I'm… fine."

Using her elbow, she punched the button.

The doors slid open and she scooted inside, dashing at cheeks that were suddenly wet. She ran a finger over the beautiful script of her name and suppressed the sob rising up her throat. "Go ahead. Tell me who the match is."

The elevator wasn't going anywhere. Bracing the box against the wall, she fumbled in her pocket for the key that would take her to the penthouse. Before she found it, Aidan stepped in.

Rory's voice sounded far away. "Beatrice won't like if I tell you."

Aidan filled the space, sucking the air away from her as he met her eyes, a frown creasing his forehead. In his hand, he held a universal key, so he could go to any floor at anytime. He slid it in the penthouse slot.

The doors closed and they rose. Aidan didn't move, his eyes still locked on hers.

"Can you text me that information?" Bree sputtered. Abruptly, she disconnected and took a step back, only to be pinned by the glass wall.

Aidan reached out and brushed a hair from her cheek. "What's wrong?"

Everything. She shifted the box into her arms. "Nothing."

"You ran out of there like your ass was on fire, and you're crying. That's not nothing."

"I got something in my eye."

That knowing tilt of his head. "I think it's time we talked."

Her phone, still in her hand, buzzed and she nearly dropped it again. *Tech Support* lit the screen with an incoming text.

It was a picture. Only a picture. But when she glanced down and saw who it was, her stomach bottomed out.

Chills swept her skin, burning nausea rose in her throat.

Russia. Interrogations. Dark, dank cells. Days without food or water.

"You're right." Swallowing a whole new set of fears, she held up the phone so Aidan could see it. His face blanched and he took a step back. "We definitely need to talk."

FOUR

A  *'no-go' area*

"It's him, isn't it?" Bree demanded, blowing past Aidan when the doors opened. She marched into the suite to the beautiful mahogany table near the balcony, slamming the box down on it before whirling to face him.

"Etienne Chardy is really Henri Moreau. He had plastic surgery to change his appearance so no one could find him, didn't he?"

Of course she'd figured it out. He should've known better than to try and get anything past her. Stepping off the elevator before the doors closed, he ran a hand through his hair. It had been one hell of the day, and it wasn't over. "I can explain."

Fury flooded her face like a torrent. Behind her, the storm lashed at the windows. "*Explain?* How? How could you pretend you didn't know who he was and lie to me?"

"He's not the same man you remember, and he had a good reason for what he did to us."

"There is no good reason." Her anger was so palpable, he expected the top of her head to explode. "He's a traitor! He blew my cover and gave me up to Boris and his comrades. Then he convinced you to trade yourself for me!"

Aidan stayed on the other side of the room just in case she started throwing things and raised his hands in a supplicating gesture. "Henri—Etienne—was trying to save his family. His wife and son were being held by Vaslov. The information he traded for their lives included you. He believed he had no choice, and in his circumstances, I would've done the same. His kid had leukemia and Vaslov was prepared to let him die. If anyone was threatening you and our child, I would've given up every goddamn spy in the world to save you."

Her retort seemed to get hung up in her mouth, anger draining from her face. After a moment, she shook her head. "No. You would've found a way without anyone else getting hurt."

Bree thought she knew him, and when it came to her safety, and what he felt for her, he *would* do anything to protect her. Had proven that by what he'd done to save her from that Russian prison, working with Chardy to make the trade. And while they had no children—yet, anyway—the imaginary son or daughter in this scenario felt uncannily real to him. It was something he wanted, a family, and he wanted it with Bree.

"I know you want to believe the best of me, and always end up thinking the worst, but in that situation, I would have done exactly what he did. There's nothing I wouldn't do to keep you safe."

Her face was grim. "Guess you've already proven that to be true."

Everything about her became very still and contained. All

of the previous animation turned off like a light switch. He could see it in her eyes—she was back in Russia, in that cell, wondering what the next torture would be.

He hadn't had the chance to speak to her before trading himself. Even after the US made a deal for him—thanks to her—and secured his rescue, the most he and Bree had discussed about it was her slapping his face and calling him a moron for making the deal. She hated owing anybody anything, especially her life, and she'd claimed to have nearly lost her mind when she realized what he'd done. She'd never admitted it, but he knew she had demanded incessantly that their boss, the head of Operations, as well as the director of the CIA, do whatever it took to get him released. She hadn't stopped, refused to sleep or eat, until they gained permission from the President of the United States to release a Russian spy in exchange for Aidan.

If it hadn't been for her, he'd still be in prison, or dead and left to rot somewhere in Siberia.

He took a tentative step toward her, hands still raised. She was like a cornered animal he didn't want to spook. "It's a complicated situation. How about we sit and talk about it?"

Her eyes snapped to the present and she crossed her arms. "You lied to me, Aidan. How can I trust you to tell me the truth now?"

"Chardy is no danger to you. He no longer works for French Intelligence—he defected to the States over a year ago."

"Did he betray his own country as well?"

Another step. "He sold secrets, yes, and is wanted by the French for that reason."

"So we took him in? The French are allies. Why would…?"

Understanding dawned and she grabbed her forehead. "The Russians aren't the only ones he's sold secrets to. The US granted him amnesty in exchange for information. He sold out his country to the Russians, and now to us. Perfect."

"He's trying to make up for what he did to you and the others. When Vaslov took his wife and child, the French refused to help him. He had no recourse but to turn on them."

He could see her turning the words over. She wanted to rage, be indignant and self-righteous, but she was beginning to understand the horrible predicament Chardy had found himself in. When you gave your all to your country and then felt the sting of betrayal when you needed their help, it made you do things you never dreamed you were capable of.

Bree stood in front of the patio window, the dark, rolling clouds outside mimicking her mood. Shadows crept from the corners of the room, threatening to hide her face from him. He went to a lamp on the side table and turned it on. "You have every reason to be angry with me for not being honest, but Chardy's situation is very delicate. We have to keep his new identity intact. He has too many people after him, too many countries trying to kill him. You have to swear to me not to tell anyone, especially whoever you're working for."

Her eyes widened slightly, and his stomach sank.

The photo of Chardy when he was still Moreau—she'd run his current face through some type of recognition program and got a hit. That's how she knew who he really was.

"Shit," he said under his breath. "They already know, don't they?"

She uncrossed her arms and leaned on the table, her chest moving in a deep sigh. "Why do you know all of this about him? About his new identity, his defection?" Not waiting for his reply, she stared at him with incomprehension. "You're working for them again, aren't you? You're working for the CIA and running operations from here in the hotel."

There was coffee in the glass carafe. His cup from that morning still sat on the sink, unmoved. He walked over and stuck it in the microwave. A headache had set up behind his eyes, and a jolt of caffeine would do him good. Besides, it would buy time to figure out exactly what he could tell her.

"I don't believe it," she said, her voice filled with exasperation. "You went back to them after what they did to me?"

He planted his hands on each side of the sink and hung his head. Of course she would see this as a betrayal. "I don't work for the Agency"—*technically*—"I work here, for your uncle."

She stomped toward him. "Bullshit. You're using this place as a cover. Tell me the truth, Aidan, or I will have you fired on the spot. And after that? I will personally kick your ass all the way back to Langley and deposit you on their doorstep."

Reluctantly, he turned and faced her.

She wasn't kidding; she now wore her spy face, the one that said he was dead meat.

Aidan had faced down vengeful terrorists, gone deep undercover with the worst of the worst, and survived torture in a Russian prison. The only thing—the only *person*—who'd ever truly inspired fear in him, outside a couple of his SEAL instructors, was the spitfire now standing in front of him with her hands on her hips.

Her glare was full of ferocious love for her uncle and the betrayal burning in her blood. He understood all of it, and she might follow through on that threat just for spite, but mostly because she believed she was protecting Martin and the DeMarco business.

"I'm sorry," he said. "You know I can't tell you about my job or the mission."

Her hand flew out to slap him, but he anticipated it, grabbing her by the wrist before she made contact. "What I can tell you," he ground out as the microwave dinged, "is that my position here in no way endangers your uncle or the Gulf Breeze."

She tried to wrestle free from his grip, *tried* being the key word. Her resistance was half-hearted as if she didn't really want him to let go of her. "I don't believe that for one second."

"It's true." He released her, slowly, savoring the delicious feel of her skin and wanting more. "I swear it."

That gave her pause. She might not trust him, but she knew he was a man of his word. He saw her throat work as she swallowed hard. "Regardless, it has to stop. If you're working for the CIA, you have to quit this job and leave."

Her demands were reasonable. Didn't matter. He couldn't leave. Not yet. "I have to see this assignment through, and your uncle won't want me to leave."

Her voice rose with self-righteousness. "He will when I tell him what you've been doing!"

Aidan knew better than to admit anything. He was sworn to absolute secrecy. His ass would be obliterated if he screwed this mission up, but she already knew the key player involved. All it would take to ruin everything would be her telling someone—anyone—in the spy community.

Might already be too late. She'd sent someone the picture of Chardy and they'd used face rec software. If whoever was on the other end put two and two together...

The clock was now ticking. He really had no choice.

"He already knows."

Silence, filled with confusion. Her brows drew down, then, "*What?*"

The incredulity in that word made it more of an expletive than a question.

"This is a delicate mission and highly, *highly* confidential, but I went to Martin and he granted permission to use the spa for...it."

She started for the elevator. "I'm going to kill him."

"Wait." He reached out and grabbed her arm to stop her.

She lost her balance and collided with him, falling into his chest. "Oh, don't worry," she said, straightening before smacking his hand away, "I'm going to kill you too."

She looked up at him then, those beautiful golden eyes he loved. There was fire behind them, ferocious and all-consuming. He needed to calm her down, find common ground. "Can you give me twenty-four hours?"

"You've got to be joking."

He shook his head, breathing deeply to fill his nostrils with her scent. "I'm serious, Bree. That's all I need. I'll finish my mission, Chardy will be gone, and the spa will go back to being completely normal. I'll hand in my resignation the minute this is over."

She stilled, not moving from him, and he saw her bite the inside of her bottom lip. Her gaze was still fierce, raking over his face, her mind spinning as she considered his offer.

Did she really want him to leave? Something told him, no. She was pissed and reacting emotionally. Not her usual style, but he seemed to be able to bring that side out of her whenever they were together. He pushed every one of her buttons—even those she'd kept buried for years—and he told himself it would be a good idea to sleep with his wits about him tonight. She might make good on the promise to kill him.

She stopped chewing on her lip and her body became fluid again, her chin rising in defiance. "On one condition."

Shit. He was in deep trouble now, he could feel it in his bones. This was worse than being killed in his sleep. "What?"

Her lips parted and a slow, faint smile spread. "Let me help you."

He barked a laugh. Now who was joking? "First of all, no. Secondly, *hell* no. Thirdly, you hate the CIA, so why would you want in? And on top of *all* that, I couldn't even if I wanted to."

"I'm pretty sure you can do whatever the hell you want since you seem to be in charge of this undercover op."

Deep shit, indeed. He chuckled at her incredible ability to assess the situation and nail the truth in mere seconds. "It's too risky."

"From my perspective, you don't have any choice. You want me to stay quiet about who Chardy really is? This is the only way it's going to happen."

God save him. This was a disaster.

Worse, he was actually considering her proposal.

He *wanted* her to work with him on the complex, slow-drip espionage operation. Wanted her to understand that Henri Moreau, aka Etienne Chardy, was actually helping the US document and expose a sophisticated Russian spy ring, run by none other than the man who'd gotten away from them last time—Boris Vaslov.

But he didn't want her to know how much he could use her help, how much he wanted her working as a partner. Not yet.

"Why did that box of ornaments make you cry?"

The change in subject threw her for a loop. "What?"

He hitched a thumb over his shoulders. "Were they your mom's?"

She whipped her head to look at the table. "They're mine," she said after a moment. "She gave some of them to me, the others we made together. I haven't seen that box since..."

All the fight went out of her and she slumped. He touched her shoulder. "I'm sorry. I should have left them in storage. I didn't know."

Her eyes were bright with tears when she glanced back at him. "No, I'm glad you found it. I...I'll go through them tonight. They'll bring back good memories. Thank you."

He couldn't help himself. He loved every inch of her. Always had. He loved the fiery Bree and this soft, vulnerable

Bree even more. He took her chin in his fingers, tilted her face up, and brought his lips down to hers.

YOU CAN'T CONTROL everything

THIS WAS COMPLETELY and utterly unacceptable.

Yet, Bree found she couldn't free herself from Aidan's magnetic kiss. His hands were gentle, solid, as they held her arms, but it didn't matter—it was like invisible grips held her in place. She couldn't break free.

Didn't *want* to break free.

His tongue traced her lips, parted them, and she heard herself sigh into his mouth. Her body melted and he pulled her into him, wrapping his arms around her.

All her worries—about him, Henri Moreau, SFI, even Megan and the damn flowers—became like air, floating away. Her mind was a blank, the sensations in her body pure bliss.

It had been too long since she'd experienced Aidan's touch. Much too long since she'd let herself relax in his competent hands. Forever since she'd tuned out the churning, over-analyzing parts of her brain in favor of feeling.

One of his hands moved up her spine, a slow, delicious teasing heat. As his tongue swept deeply into her mouth, that hand gripped the back of her neck, his thumb massaging the taut muscles there.

She was angry, so, so angry. At him, the CIA, Henri Moreau. She was even angry at the Russians. Uncle Martin. Everything was wrong, out of her control.

Especially Aidan. She thrust her tongue into his mouth as if to tell him so. She hated being out-of-control, hated the anger burning like a flame inside her. But it was mixed with something else, something that only Aidan seemed able to ignite.

If he was working for the CIA again, there was no way she'd be able to convince him to go to work for Shadow Force instead. Her mission was a bust, *damn him.*

Without a successful mission, she had nothing to go back to Beatrice with. She might as well stay and run the spa.

Kill me now.

Sometimes it felt like the world was conspiring against her. That she was fighting a war she could never win, and she was so damn tired.

Aidan's mouth broke from hers, his lips trailing kisses along her jaw line, to her earlobe. His strong hands felt good, as if he were hanging onto her in a way that kept the world at bay, pushing that invisible war she was always fighting with herself away. "God, I've missed you."

The tight band around her chest eased. "Why?"

He pulled back slightly to look into her eyes, a question there. "Why? Because I haven't touched you in almost two years."

"You have Megan."

His brows slammed together. "What are you talking about?"

"It's okay." She tried to keep her voice steady, failed. He truly seemed confused. "The flowers? I heard her and Candace talking. I know you sent them to her."

He threw his head back and laughed heartily. "There's nothing going on between us, although she'd like there to be. The flowers are a long story, but Cliff notes, I nearly killed her this morning. She doesn't like chocolate, and I don't know her well enough beyond that to know what she does like, so I sent a simple holiday arrangement to say I'm sorry. That's all."

"Oh." It had sure seemed like more, but she couldn't blame

Megan for pining after Aidan. Even though he irritated the snot out of her, she found she didn't want him interested in another woman. Selfish of her, for sure, considering how poorly she'd treated him.

She studied his face, spreading her hands over his chest. Underneath her palm she could feel the strong heartbeat. "Why would you miss me when I'm such a bitch? I've treated you like crap."

His confusion seemed to deepen. "That road runs both ways. I haven't exactly been a supportive husband."

Her voice came out raspy. "You traded yourself for me. You saved my life. I never even said thank you."

"I would do the same again."

So matter-of-fact. That was that. He didn't even have to think about it.

This was so not the time to discuss their relationship, or what had happened in Russia, and yet every time she opened her mouth, that's where she went. "I wouldn't let you. I shouldn't have then, but...thank you. What you did for me, I'll never forget it."

A knowing smile. "Then, you'll never forget me, no matter how long you stay away, or how far you run."

He was still holding onto her, anchoring her and keeping her worries from devouring her like they usually did. His lips had been so soft, so gentle. She wanted to touch them with her fingertips, outline them with her tongue.

Shaking started in her body, first in her chest, making her heartbeat jump and skip. It spread down her arms, her fingers. One of her hands slid over his white shirt, up his neck, finding the pulse there. Her throat burned with more words than she should say, more apologies, but she squeezed her eyes shut. There was still anger in her, but underneath that, fear. Just like when she discovered he'd traded himself, that he was going to endure torture and pain at the hands of Boris Vaslov, possibly death, because of her.

Fear was harder to deal with, anger was a good friend.

But right now, the anger was a slow burn, not the hot flame she needed to push him away. She wanted to bring him closer, feel his heat, banish that fear.

He had survived Vaslov; she had as well. Years before, he'd been there to obliterate her fear, her grief, after her mother died. He blotted it all away.

He had that skill, even now. As she opened her eyes, she saw the look on his face, beckoning her to abandon it and let him stoke a different fire.

But why? "You didn't answer my question."

He knew what she was asking, knew the words she wanted to hear, even if she wouldn't believe them. "Yes, I have. You know damn well why I've done the things I have for you, why I would again. I love you, Bree McNamara. I've loved you from the moment I saw you, and I will never stop, even when they put me in the grave."

The shaking spread to her belly, down her legs. "That's the part I don't understand. Why me? Why would you"—*anyone* —"love me?"

He quirked his head. "You're the most beautiful, intelligent, amazing woman I've ever met. Why wouldn't I be head over heels in love with you?"

Her parents and Uncle Martin were the only ones who'd ever loved her. At least that she could remember. Both grandparents had died when she was too little to recall them; and even her father had died in the line of duty when she was only seven. Her memories of him were fuzzy, her mother becoming her lifeline at such a young age.

Aidan ran a finger along her jawline, down her neck. Tiny sparks ignited along her spine, her body very aware of the hand that rested on her lower back. "I just wish you loved me back."

I do. She wanted to say the words, but they stuck in her throat, her mouth working in silence. "You righted my world more than once, and I will always appreciate that, truly I do, but you betrayed me in the field. We had a plan to handle that Russian spy ring and you went over my head with Moreau—Chardy—and blew the entire mission."

Shutters came down over his eyes, but his voice was still caring as he said, "What happened with the Russians was a bad call on my part and I wish I could take it back. All I can do is try to make it up to you and my country."

"Is that what you're doing now? Trying to correct past damage by working with the Agency on whatever this under-cover mission is?"

"I would do anything for you, anytime, anywhere. That will never change. "

Except tell her about his current operation or why he was working for the CIA again. "You're dodging my question. Did you ever actually leave, or was that a lie too? Have you been working for them all this time?"

A deep sigh, a wry smile. "It's one mission, Bree, that's all. I do this and I'm done. I work for your uncle, and I will continue to do so after this, unless you want me to leave. Like I said before, I'll pack my bags and go if you just give me twenty-four hours to see this through. I'll..." He hesitated as if it pained him to say the next words. "I'll sign the divorce papers. I'll promise to never cross your path again."

One mission. One terribly important mission if he was willing to agree to all of that.

What would make him give up on their marriage? Her heart did another skip, but this one in fear. Fear of losing him, never seeing him again.

"Why you?" she asked. "What makes you the expert on this particular assignment that they couldn't find someone else to do it?"

He didn't answer, his gaze falling to her lips, as if memorizing their shape, their taste. "I'm sorry. I can't tell you that."

He didn't have to. Sudden insight made her catch her breath, take a step back. He let her, his arms falling open, hands landing on her elbows. "Bree—"

"It's the Russians, isn't it?" she demanded. "It's the spy ring, round two. You and Moreau—Chardy, I mean. You're both going after them again."

His lips firmed—her only answer.

"Holy shit! They're here?" Her stomach threatened to bottom out. "What the hell are they doing in Texas?"

The spy ring they'd gone after during their joint tenure in the CIA had been seeded twenty years ago in a small suburb of Arlington, VA. She and Aidan had been nearly five thousand miles away in Moscow when they'd discovered the spy ring's plans.

"There's no one you need to worry about in this location. You and your uncle are safe."

In *this* location.

Safe was relative.

While Aidan had an uncanny ability to make her feel safe, knowing he was working to uncover the same spy ring, the same basic mission to track them down, terrified her. "Are you crazy?" Vaslov's face flashed across her mind, her stomach now cramping. "They know who you are! Besides the fact you can't run a sanctioned CIA mission on US soil..."

He released her completely and held her accusatory gaze without so much as blinking.

"It isn't sanctioned," she said, her stomach finally hitting the floor. "They brought you in to run an unsanctioned mission, knowing you would do it to make up for the goatfuck that happened in Russia, and if you fail, they'll deny any involvement."

Not a hint of confirmation. Not a hint of emotion. Nothing showed on his face or in his eyes. "You're jumping to a lot of conclusions."

"Well, here's one more for you. We're practically sitting on the Mexican border, so my guess is this group of Russian spies is sneaking over the border and you know where, when, and how many. You've been following them, seeing where they end up, and your new friend, Chardy, is here to work the final sting...getting them to come out of hiding. What's he offering them? What kind of intelligence?"

Stoic silence.

"Goddammit, Aidan. Talk to me. Tell me what the hell is going on."

He reached out to touch her cheek. "You worry too much. Everything's fine."

She jerked back. "The hell it is. If something goes sideways, you could end up branded a traitor. Or in prison right here in the good ol' US of A. Or worse, dead."

He skirted around her, heading for the elevator. "I see your confidence in me is as high as ever." He punched the button and the doors opened. Two steps and he was inside. "Do you remember who trained me?"

Frustrated beyond measure, she placed her balled fists on her hips and marched over to face him, planting her feet. "I did."

"One of the best in the business." That wry smile surfaced. "And in that case, you should know you have nothing to worry about."

He winked.

The doors slid shut on his grin.

FIVE

Never stop thinking about ways to solve a problem

THE ELEVATOR WAS ABOUT to start its descent, Aidan's lips still tingling with the feel of Bree's mouth, when the doors slid open and she barreled into the space, knocking him backward.

"You don't get to do that," she said, hitting the stop button and squaring her shoulders. Her eyes sparked with anger and arousal. "You don't get to dump all that on me and just leave."

"I know it's a lot, Bree, but—"

The next thing he knew, she threw herself at him, her lips cutting off his words.

His body reacted instinctively, throwing up a *hell yeah*. His arms went around her, crushing her to his chest and lifting her off the ground.

It was like the homecoming kiss she'd given him when he'd finally made it back to the States. During his time in the Navy, he'd seen friends and comrades receive these kinds of welcomes from wives and girlfriends, but there'd never been that type of welcome home for him. As a SEAL, his returns had usually been under the radar. Same when he was a spy.

Except for one.

He'd been hobbled with a broken ankle, the wounds from the torture he'd survived still fresh. The medical care he'd received on the flight home had been extensive but he'd barely been able to make it off the C-17 transport plane without being carried. It had taken every ounce of grit he had to stand and walk down those steps.

But he had. He'd come home with his head up and his dignity intact.

Seeing what waited for him on the tarmac had made the pain of maneuvering the steps worth it. Sunlight had caught in Bree's coppery hair as it blew in the breeze. She'd sprinted across the distance, shoving at the hands that tried to hold her back away, and jumped into his arms.

She'd nearly felled him, her weight and momentum threatening to collapse his ankle, even with the air cast boot. But my God, the feel of her in his arms...

Just like now. In that prison, all he'd thought about was holding her, kissing her. For the past two years, he'd gone down that same rabbit hole over and over again, never able to get her out of his mind, from under his skin.

Whirling her around, he trapped her against the wall of the elevator, deep diving with his tongue into her generous mouth. Her tongue teased his, her fingers raked through his short hair. One leg wrapped around his thigh as she arched to meet his ardent kiss.

His lips moved to her neck, teeth nipping her earlobe before slipping lower, drawing a moan from her throat. She tipped her head, granting access, her light floral perfume teasing his nostrils. "Oh, Aidan," she whispered. "I'm so sorry."

He held her tight, anchoring her hips against him as he dropped his lips to her collarbone, the dip of her satin dress between her breasts. Her hips bucked, her hands gripped his shirt lapels, ran down his ribs.

Her skin was creamy and soft, his tongue making light swirls over the swelling mounds peeking above the material. He cupped the underside of one luscious mound, pressing it up, his tongue sliding under the material, licking her through the gauzy fabric of her bra.

She gasped and he flicked his tongue over her pert nipple, ready to carry her back into the suite. He wanted his first time with her after their drought to be special, memorable. Not some quickie—although, God knew his body was like a pubescent teenager and that might be the best he could manage—against the inside of an elevator. He wanted to strip her down slowly, relish every inch of skin, make her beg for more.

Beep, beep, beep.

The alarm cut through the daze he felt, lost in her body. After sixty seconds of being stopped, the elevator always sounded a warning.

"What is...that?" she breathed, her voice low and throaty.

"Nothing." He kept giving her light, quick kisses. In the security office, Joey was probably getting his rocks off watching from the hidden camera. "Don't worry about it."

He hit the button to release it and the doors closed behind them.

But the mood was broken, at least for Bree, and Aidan's nightmare came crashing back. "What am I doing?" she remarked, drawing away from him. Her fingers covered her lips, her head shaking in disbelief. "What the hell am I doing?"

Shit. Here came the overthinking, the self-loathing.

"Kissing your husband," he said, "and making him a very happy man."

She walked toward the table with the box sat, bracing her hands as she stared out the window. "This isn't like me."

It struck him the wrong way. "Isn't it? I seem to recall a weekend in Vegas when you were trying to numb yourself and we ended up married. I'd like to believe my charm had something to do with that, but you have to admit, you're good at jumping first and asking questions later."

He expected her to whirl around with a sarcastic retort, but she kept her back to him. One of her hands toyed with the lid of the box. "We're still on for dinner, right?"

How many times could she surprise him in one day?

Don't look a gift horse in the mouth. He did a mental fist pump. "Whatever you want, I'm at your disposal."

Her phone buzzed and she answered without turning to look at him. "Yes?" There was a slight pause. "Oh sure. I'm a little tied up at the moment, but I'll be there shortly."

Finally, she faced him. "Loretta is done with the flower arranging, and Megan wants me to check the decorations before the group calls it quits."

"Guess that's my cue to leave then." He punched the elevator button once more and the doors slid open. "I'll see you at seven."

She didn't offer to ride down with him, which disappointed him, but he knew she needed to work through whenever the hell was going on with her. She was pissed about him working for the CIA again, and the mission. He wished he could bring her in on it; she knew the players even better than he did. It was late in the game, though. Too late to get clearance or change the plan.

Bree would never go for it anyway. While she certainly might want to help him stop Vaslov and his new spy ring—and maybe exact a little revenge for both of them—her distrust and anger at the Agency would keep her from fully participating. He knew her, regardless of their estrangement. She claimed to want to be in on it, but he suspected her motives included a little revenge on the Agency as well.

He understood that motivation, even though he didn't share it. The CIA did a lot of crappy things, but they also did some incredible things to keep the country safe. As a former SEAL, he'd done the same.

Aidan just hoped Bree never found out the real reason the CIA had retired her. If she did, the torture he'd survived in Russia would be nothing compared to what she'd do to him.

ON THE TAKE

THE MINUTE AIDAN LEFT, Bree returned Rory's call. "Sorry about that. I had company."

"Figured as much. What do you want me to do? Is that your guy or not?"

She stood at the patio doors watching the storm. Fog rolled in off the water, and the rain drenched everything. A diehard beachcomber walked the sand in a yellow slicker and boots. Waves rolled up high on the beach, one right after the other. "No," she lied, "but the photo you sent—I knew him back in my Agency days. This guest reminded me of him, that's all."

Rory had probably already made the connection, but she hoped he'd drop it anyway. He had dozens of missions on his plate he was running intel for. Most likely, he would be happy to let this one go, especially since it was not part of her assignment. "You need anything else, then?"

Bree pulled the keycard she'd lifted from Aidan out of her dress pocket and examined it. It was a master that could open any door in the place. She wasn't sure how long she had before he figured out it was missing, so she had to move quickly. "I need a little help blocking some security cameras."

Rory chuckled. "Do I want to know why?"

She tossed the keycard on the table and touched her lips. They tingled from Aidan's ardent kisses. "It would be better if you don't."

She heard the tap of fingers on a keyboard. "Your uncle's system is closed circuit. If you want help from my end, you have to get me in first."

It was a risk, since he'd have to report to Beatrice eventually, but she had to know what Chardy was planning. Regardless if Aidan wanted her help or not, she had to watch his back. Chardy could not be trusted. "How do I do that?"

She listened carefully as he explained, and then she left her room and went to work.

At six-thirty, Bree tapped the SFI app on her phone and caused the camera in the hallway outside Aidan's room to malfunction. She knew from Joey that Aidan was showering before their dinner. She needed two minutes to sneak in and replace the keycard in his jacket.

Thanks to Rory's help, she'd managed to avoid the cameras and get into Chardy's suite to plant several listening devices while the man was downstairs getting a massage. She'd even plugged a USB into his laptop and downloaded the contents. Later tonight, she'd review the files and make sure there was nothing suggesting he was double crossing Aidan or the CIA. She still wanted to clone his phone, but he'd taken that with him, so it would have to wait.

For now, she needed to return the keycard and slip back out without notice if possible. Joey and Aidan had been preoccupied during her snooping, trying to figure out what was wrong with the security cameras, and she hoped between that and everything that had happened with her and Aidan earlier today, he was too distracted to notice his key was missing.

She pressed an ear against the door to his room. The muffled sounds of a shower running filtered through, along with noise from a television. She continued to listen for another moment, trying to catch the fall of footsteps or anything to suggest he was not in the bathroom. Reassured he was indeed occupied, she knocked lightly. When there was no response, she slipped the keycard in and was rewarded when the light turned green.

The room was sparse, light from the basketball game on the TV dancing across the bed. He'd always been a neat freak, probably because of his days in the Navy, and she was surprised to see his jacket and pants casually thrown on the unmade bed.

His phone was next to a closed laptop and some files on the desk across from a sitting area. Two pairs of shoes sat by the door, several suits and casual shirts hung in the half open closet. On the floor rested a dry cleaning bag filled to the brim.

As she tiptoed to his jacket on the bed, a photo on the nightstand caught her attention. She stopped in mid-slink, breath catching in her chest.

There were the two of them grinning at the camera as they held up their ring fingers. The matching bands were cheap ones Aidan had found in a souvenir store. He'd promised to buy her a real one as soon as he returned from his next mission, but she hadn't cared. She'd been drunk and hurting over the loss of her mom. He'd been a knight in shining armor, sweeping her off her feet and making her laugh instead of cry. The weekend had been a whirlwind, the first time she'd let go in so long.

Monday had come too fast, and she'd wanted to stay in Vegas, pretend she didn't have to go back and deal with her mother's will, handle the world without her biggest supporter.

All of it came crashing back in that moment as she stood frozen in the middle of the room. She still hadn't looked through the box of ornaments Aidan had found. While she knew every last one of them, she wanted to wait until she had a moment to herself before she went through them. The memories were old, but the deep grief was always right there, close to the surface, and there was no opening that box without tapping into that grief once more.

In the years since, Aidan had been the only one to numb it, to keep it at bay. Bree always threw herself into her work when the grief demon raised its ugly head, but the truth was, the only time she'd found relief was in Aidan's arms.

It had been a ridiculous fool's game to marry him in Vegas, and she'd filed an annulment, but it had never gone through. Before she could straighten anything out, he'd gone dark—a SEAL mission had taken him out of the country for weeks. When he returned, she was out of the country on her own mission for the Agency. Along the way, they never seemed to connect long enough to file for divorce, and the couple times she'd hunted him down to try and talk about it, he'd always ended up making her laugh and believing their marriage might stand a chance.

And then after the death of a close friend on a mission in Syria, Aidan left the SEALs. It was her turn to comfort him and she'd done it out of a sense of duty, as well as love.

But they were more different than alike, and acting as a

married couple ended up with them fighting all the time. He'd stayed on the West Coast and she'd gone to the East, not seeing him for months. When he'd shown up at the Farm for training, she'd nearly lost it. What the hell was he thinking?

She couldn't protect him, couldn't fail him, and within a few months they were both in Russia.

Fishing the band on the necklace out from between her breasts, she held it for a moment wishing she could go back to that weekend. There was so damn much pain between them, she'd convinced herself the only thing they truly shared was grief. The only times when they weren't fighting had been when they were nursing each other through it. You couldn't build a strong marriage on that, could you?

She shook her head, returning the necklace to its hiding spot. Creeping the rest of the way to the bed, she bent forward and slid the keycard into the inside breast pocket of Aidan's jacket. The scent of his cologne wafted up to her nose, the memory of his lips and hands sending heat through her.

She had no idea what might happen during their dinner, and she still planned to recruit him for Beatrice, but it didn't stop her from being worried about him. The CIA, Chardy, the Russians... who was playing who in this scenario?

Still bent over and stroking the jacket, she froze mentally and cursed when she heard the bathroom door open, the sound of the shower getting louder.

She felt his presence behind her left shoulder and bit her bottom lip.

"Is there something I can help you with, darling? If you're that eager to get in my bed, you should've said something sooner."

Slowly, she glanced at him over her shoulder and straightened. Goosebumps ran over her skin at the sight of him in nothing more than a towel as he leaned on the doorjamb.

Her eyes widened and words escaped her. He was every bit as buff as he'd been in the SEALs, as sexy as the last time she'd seen him naked. The beautiful muscles, the flat belly, the tattoos that covered his chest and arms.

She blinked once, then again. This is what got her in trouble. She'd confront him, planning to get her way about something, and then he'd smile, kiss her silly, and take off his clothes.

It just wasn't fair.

He pushed off the door frame and sauntered across the room toward her. His hair was damp and he smelled fresh and clean. He brushed against her as he leaned over to grab the jacket. His fingers fished into the breast pocket and brought out the keycard. He held it under her nose, looking down into her eyes with a smirk on his face. "Sure you don't need more time to spy on our guest?"

"I, uh..." She swallowed hard. "You knew?"

He tossed the jacket and the key card onto the bed. "I wanted to believe it was my charm that made you attack me in the elevator, but once a spy always a spy, right?"

Damn. "I only did it because I'm worried, Aidan."

He wrapped his arms around her and drew her close. "I know. Plus, you're just damn nosy."

Her brain blanked with her head resting against his chest, his heartbeat filling her ear. The temptation to rip off the towel was so great she could hardly swallow. "You're not going to yell at me?"

He chuckled and she felt it through her whole system. "I've found that tactic to be ineffective with you." His fingers locked around both her wrists. "I've decided instead to tie you up and keep you in my room until the mission is over."

SIX

Mission Impossible

THE LOOK on Bree's face was priceless. She gasped and tried to jerk away. "Let go of me."

He held on and hustled her to a chair before gently shoving her into it. "I'm kidding, but don't push it, or I *will* until I take out this spy ring."

Her gold eyes pleaded with him. "A, I want to help."

He had a weakness for those eyes, that look. He felt it all the way to his toes. As if she knew, her gaze dropped to his lower half and his cock gave a little kick. He saw her bite the inside of her lip.

Standing there in nothing but a towel, it was a struggle to keep his mind off her full mouth and what it had done to certain parts of his anatomy in the past. His body urged him to snatch her up and bend her over the table—she'd seemed willing enough earlier, but then again, maybe she just wanted to steal his keycard.

That was always the problem—he never knew for sure what she was after, hiding, or how she felt about him. Part of it was the fact she's been trained as a spy, the other because she simply didn't share herself with anyone. She'd admitted that to him long ago. After she lost her mother, who was also her best friend, she never believed she could find anyone she could love and trust as much. Not even her Uncle Martin, whom she adored. She'd admitted it was a flaw in her system, one she couldn't get over no matter how she tried.

He moved heaven and hell to prove to her she could trust him, and done everything he could to try and understand this quirk in her personality. After all the psychological training as a spy, he believed it had something to do with her father and the fact he'd died when she was only seven. He and Bree's mother apparently had fallen in love at first sight and enjoyed an amazing marriage until the Marine was killed in action. Aidan believed it wasn't so much that Bree didn't trust people, she simply didn't trust life not to snatch away those she loved, unexpectedly.

She came out of the chair and stood right in front of him. She'd changed into another dress, this one a deep purple, and four inch heels. She was still a good six inches shorter than him and he held still as he looked down into her eyes, her hands tracing over the tattoo on his chest. "Please, Aidan. I don't trust Moreau, and you shouldn't either. I have a team with considerable skills and resources outside the CIA that I can call on to help make sure you don't get burned by him or the Agency. I won't interfere with whatever you have planned, just let me do some digging and back you up."

She smelled like flowers and cinnamon, her fingers light

and teasing on his pecs. It was hard to concentrate. "Who do you work for now?"

"An independent group that specializes in everything from paramilitary operations to undercover missions here in the states and abroad."

"Sanctioned by the government?"

Her gaze dropped to his chest and she gave a little shrug. "Some."

Meaning most weren't.

"We help people who have nowhere else to turn," she continued. "Those in sticky situations with the government, others who can't go to traditional law enforcement for help or protection."

It was all he could do not to touch her. Doing so might break the spell. "Does this organization have a name?"

"Are you going to let me help you?"

Everything was a negotiation with her. "Is the name top-secret?"

"The organization is, and the specific group I work for within it is at an even higher level."

Damn. He had a feeling she was telling the truth. "Why did they send you?"

Her fingers trailed down the center of his chest, to his belly button, then to the top of the towel, making him suck in his breath. "Why do you think? I just came to see Uncle Martin."

That was a lie, and she was using the art of distraction to cover it. He grabbed hold of her wrist to stop her from touching his hip bone where the towel was slung low. "Tell me who they are and why they sent you."

Her gaze came back up to meet his, hard and calculating. "I planned to all along but knowing that you're working for the Agency again changes my plan."

"I told you, it's one mission, Bree. I'm only doing it to shut down this fucking spy ring once and for all." The pulse in her wrist was featherlight under his thumb as he stroked the tiny bones there. "The only two things that get me out of bed in the morning are the plan to save our marriage and the other to hunt down the Russian spies who got away from us the last time."

"Did I hear you right? You really want to save our marriage?"

"Yes, but I realized a while ago it's not about that anymore. Bottom line, I want you to be happy. If that means staying away from me, then I'll learn to live with it, but I'll never give up hope that someday you'll come back to me."

"Aidan, I..."

A knock at the door interrupted her and they both jumped apart. "Room service!"

"You ordered room service for dinner?" she asked. "I thought I was taking you out, that was the deal, wasn't it? I had to pay?"

He headed for the bathroom, figuring he better get dressed. "If you want in on the operation, then dinner is served here tonight."

She stood there, looking slightly stunned. "You planned this all along, didn't you?"

He grinned at her over his shoulder in the bathroom doorway. "Could you get it? I don't want to answer it in just a towel."

Her eyes dropped to the towel again and he chuckled before he closed the door behind him.

When he emerged a few minutes later, the table was set with a feast of steak, lobster, French fries—her favorite—and two gourmet Caesar salads, a bottle of champagne chilling in a bucket of ice next to the table. She sat in a chair, one long leg crossed over the other and her shoes kicked off near the bed.

She was on her cell, but upon seeing him, she ended the conversation and tucked the phone away.

"Apparently my uncle got wind of our dinner together and sent the champagne."

The bottle had been uncorked and Aidan went to work pouring. He handed a glass to her and raised his own in salute. "To dinner between a couple of spies."

She clinked hers against his. "To profitable new partnerships between a husband and wife."

A flare of hope took root in his chest. He imagined what it would've been like if Russia had never happened. The two of them going undercover together, seeing the world, protecting their country. "I'll let you in as long as you stay out of my way, and tell me the details about this organization you work for."

She swung her crossed leg back and forth and smiled at him as if she had a secret. "Promise me you're done with the Agency after this. Cross your heart, swear on the Bible, open a vein and make a blood oath—I don't care—just swear this is your last and final mission for them, and I will tell you everything about the company I work for."

The bubbles tickled the back of his throat. She was always champagne and lobster to his beer and peanuts. Setting down his glass, he took her by the hand and drew her out of the chair, bringing her once more in front of him. Looking down into her eyes, he said, "I swear to you this is my last and final mission for the CIA."

And then he sealed it with a kiss.

She tasted like champagne and excitement. Her breasts pressed against his chest and she slipped her tongue into his mouth. They stayed that way for a long time, both exploring each other gently, as if the fragile agreement between them could be broken if they moved too fast, too recklessly.

In that moment, Aidan could shut up all the tit for tat,

negotiating, the ache that had been in his chest for the past two years, for the misery she'd put him through. Of all the women he could've picked that night in Vegas, he'd been drawn to her, and he'd never felt like this about anyone else before or since.

When they finally broke apart, she looked into his eyes and shocked him yet again.

"Shadow Force International," she whispered. "I work for their spy division, Nemesis, and I came here to recruit you, Aidan McNamara, to join us."

***

HOSTILE RECRUITMENT

AIDAN CHOKED as if he'd swallowed too much champagne and Bree smiled at the expression on his face.

Brows furrowed, he cocked his head. "Say what?"

Her body shivered from the kiss. Head to toe, she was a mess. She'd never planned to seduce him, or even get this close. It hadn't even been twenty-four hours and she was throwing herself at him.

The first time was different. She'd needed that keycard. This time? Hell, she had no clue what she was doing. She couldn't even blame it on the champagne, she'd barely had two sips.

But something about being near Aidan, especially seeing his naked chest, yearning to feel his lips again, she'd lost her ever-lovin' mind.

That's what he did to her—turned her brain to mush. Turned her body to molten lava that only he could then quench.

"You check all of the boxes," she continued softly. "Shadow

Force is made up of former SEALs, most of whom suffer from PTSD or physical disabilities and struggle to keep a nine-to-five job. Some work for the Rock Star Security division as body-guards—that's the face of the organization, the one known to the public, and it's growing faster than we can keep up with. Along with that, there are several teams who perform specialized missions, much like the SEALs—rescuing people, taking down the bad guys, the usual. The spy division, Nemesis, is new, and looking to expand. Everyone in it has training as an operative"—outside of Cassandra, anyway, but Bree couldn't focus on that at the moment— "and we work in pairs, mostly male-female, to get into places where the paramilitary division can't. Most of it is foreign work, but occasionally, we're on United States soil."

He sighed through his nose, his dark brows still lowered. "Work for who exactly?"

"Private clients and companies, sometimes, like I mentioned before, the President of the United States gets involved."

One brow rose in question. "How does the CIA feel about that?"

"Mostly, they stay out of our business and we stay out of theirs. We take on situations where they can't legally operate or lack the resources to handle it."

He was silent for a long moment, processing, no doubt, by the look in his eyes. "So you're working for a privatized version of the Agency, with no oversight or government interference, and the president uses you when she needs deniability where something could go wrong."

In a nutshell. "Like our name, we stay in the shadows as much as possible. My boss is very particular about who she hires. She wants you. There are only a handful of former SEALs who've completed spy training as well and have experience in the field. Down the road, she plans to select a few who are part of Rock Star Security and the Shadow Force teams and train them for undercover work, but right now, she needs guys like you who can hit the floor running."

Another thick silence. "You and I would be working together." There was a hint of an underlying question, as if he couldn't believe it. When she didn't immediately respond, he snickered. "You couldn't wait to get me out of DC two years ago, and now you want me to come back? Not just come back, but work as a spy with you again? Going undercover as your partner?"

There was far too much hope in his gaze. She felt horrible squashing it, but she wouldn't lie.

"Most likely not," she admitted.

"Why not? You just said it was a small group and you work in male-female pairs. We were partners before, why wouldn't we be again?"

She took a step back and motioned at the table. "We should eat. The food's getting cold."

He didn't push for a response. Joining her at the table, he seemed distracted. No surprise.

She was a vegetarian and Uncle Martin had done a great job making sure she had a delicious meat-free quiche, while Aidan enjoyed surf and turf.

They ate in silence for several minutes, and she wondered what he was thinking. He'd always been that way—a man of action, the one who thought through everything and did a thorough job of enacting it.

"The pay is excellent," she told him, "and there's a full slate of benefits. Plus, you'll be working with some of your SEAL brothers. I'm sure you won't know all of them, but you know Jaxon Sloan and Cal Reese."

His fork stopped in mid-air on the way to his mouth. "Jax works for you?"

She nodded, mentally crossing her fingers this would sway him, as she nonchalantly buttered a homemade roll. "If you can believe it, he and Ruby worked a mission together for us not too long ago. I thought they might kill each other first, but they ended up engaged after it all went down."

"Damn." He finished taking his bite and swallowed before saying, "I never imagined him as a spy."

Technically, he hadn't been; Ruby was, and together they had unraveled a mystery and stopped a terrorist while falling in love. "He's finishing his residency to become a doctor. Looks like he'll stay on the Shadow Force payroll in that capacity."

"No shit? You guys need medical care often?"

Her mind flashed back to Cassandra and her stomach roiled. She put down the uneaten roll and sat back, wiping her fingers on a napkin. "What we do is dangerous, and yes, people get hurt, but that's part of our mission. Everyone carries risk and danger, which honestly, is why so many of them love it. They also do it because putting themselves in the way of harm, in order to save someone else, gives them a purpose."

He continued to eat and nodded, encouraging her to go on if she wanted.

"You know what it's like when you leave the brotherhood, when the Agency kicks you out because you're not in top shape, you're too old, or they're just plain sick of you. What do you do then? You're highly trained, have skills far beyond the average citizen, and you can't talk about what happened to you, who you worked for, or the missions where you saved hundreds of thousands of people. You're an unsung hero and you're supposed to work for minimum wage behind the counter at a convenience store or at a desk job filling out spreadsheets.

Shadow Force gives all of us a chance to use our skills and still be of service to our country."

He looked at his plate, using his fork to move his food around. He took a couple of bites, chewed slowly, and fell back into silence.

Bree waited patiently, hoping he was considering the offer and would see the benefits in it, even if she wasn't going to be his partner. She hoped appealing to his sense of duty might help, along with knowing some of the men who already worked for SFI.

"What does Cal Reese do? Does he run one of the teams?"

It was a good sign he was asking questions. "Yes actually, he does. He's married to the boss, Beatrice, and they're friends of the founder, Emit Petit. Even though the company has been growing and expanding, everyone knows everyone. It's a tight knit group. You always have someone to help, to have your back. Not like at the Agency where you're often working totally on your own without backup."

He noticed she wasn't eating. "But you don't want to work with me."

She fiddled with the napkin, sipped the champagne, stalling. "It's not a matter of what I want. The situation is...complicated."

Setting down his fork, he picked up his drink and leaned back. "I've got all night. Tell me why it's complicated."

Okay then. "The Agency was right to retire me," she admitted quietly. "I'm not at my peak anymore, my field days are over."

He studied her with those intense eyes. "That's bullshit and you know it."

She gave a mocking laugh. "I couldn't even lift a keycard without you knowing it."

A grin crossed his face. "That's because I know you so well. I would've been disappointed if you hadn't tried."

Cocky. Sexy as hell. But too willing to let her off the hook. "You caught me sneaking in here to replace it. I'm telling you, I've lost it. Russia fucked me up. I suck as a spy now."

The grin vanished, his lips pressing into a thin line. "The Bree McNamara I know would never admit it, even if it was true."

She folded the napkin in her lap. "Maybe I'm not the same Bree you know. *Think* you know."

He sat forward, pinning her with his gaze. "If Shadow Force is so elite, why did this Beatrice gal hire you then?"

A sad smile was all she could offer. He was trying to make her feel better, confident.

"Come on, Bree. I'm not buying it." He tapped a finger on the table. "You may be a different spy than you were in Russia, but you still have the skills and know what to do. The keycard thing is a fluke. Once I knew you wouldn't let the Chardy thing drop, I anticipated you'd try to get into his room, or at least have a look at his laptop. When I knew you'd lifted it, it was only a matter of being patient for you to try and return it. I anticipated that too. None of that makes you a bad spy, it just makes me a good one."

The cockiness extended to his confidence level. Even after Russia, he had never lost that.

"It's more than the keycard and you catching me trying to return it." Her stomach was still roiling, but maybe coming clean would help. If there was one person she could admit her failings to, it was the man sitting across from her. He wouldn't judge, and if she really was a screwup, he'd be the first to tell her. "On my last assignment, I nearly got a woman killed."

"You just said it's a dangerous job. This type of work often has collateral damage, no matter how hard we try to keep innocent people safe."

"The thing is, she *was* my assignment. It wasn't my call, and honestly, I don't think she should've been involved, but she was. My one and only job was to make sure she was safe, and I failed. She's alive, but barely."

He sat back again, those keen eyes studying her face once more. "Start at the beginning."

Sharing specific details was unwise, but maybe a bargain was in the works. "Our missions are top-secret, but what I can tell you is her name is Cassandra, and she's the attorney for SFI. You'll get to meet her when you join. Recently, she was in the field to help with an extraction and insisted on going undercover to end a biological epidemic. She ended up infected with a deadly disease." The woman's heart had stopped several times, her organs trying to shut down, and Jaxon and the other doctors working on her almost couldn't revive her.

Just thinking about it made Bree shudder. "Keeping her out of trouble should've been easy, but I let myself get distracted at a key moment. She nearly died because of my incompetence."

"What the hell was a lawyer doing in the field going undercover?"

"Her parents were physicians and knew more about bacterial and viral diseases than anyone in the organization. She wanted to help stop an epidemic, and we had a solid plan to do just that and not let anyone get hurt. Things went to hell."

"I assume you did stop it?"

"Yes, and it would've been as horrible as you can imagine. Millions, maybe even billions would have died."

"But no one actually did."

She knew what he was getting at. "Cassandra nearly did and it's my fault."

"You always were too hard on yourself. Sounds to me as if

Beatrice should've kept her lawyer behind the desk where she'd be safe."

"Cassandra insisted," she argued, and then saw that one brow raise again in question.

"Then it's just as much her fault for going into the field when she doesn't have any training, and Beatrice, for letting her."

Irritated, she tossed her napkin on the table. "Regardless, it was my job to—"

He held up a hand stop her. "Fine, it's all your fault. I suspect, though, if that were true, you wouldn't be working for the anymore, would you? If Beatrice thought you were washed up, that you couldn't perform to her standards, she wouldn't have sent you here to recruit me."

He was half-right. "I'm on probation, and this is part of my current mission—to talk you into joining us."

A grin crooked the corner of his mouth again. "And if you fail?"

Before she could answer, the buzzer on her watch went off.

"What the hell is that?" Aidan asked.

It was equipped with multiple functions and apps, one being an alert to the movements of her target. She rose, snatching up her phone and activating the GPS map where a red dot now blinked. "He's on the move."

"Who?"

"Chardy. He's left the building."

Aidan stood as well, heading to the wall and running his hand behind the painting hanging there. Suddenly, a section opened and he rushed inside.

Bree followed as he asked, "You put a GPS tracker on him? How did you manage that?"

The room was tiny, nothing but a card table and the laptop. Aidan opened the latter and hit a couple keys.

"It's rainy and windy," she said. "I figured if he went anywhere he 'd throw on a jacket, so I stuck a tiny tracker under the collar."

Aidan's capable fingers tapped at the keyboard. The screen split into different views of all the building's exits. "There." He pointed to a shadowy figure disappearing into the dunes not far from the back patio. "Where the hell is he going?"

The beach was pitch black, heavy fog in the air, and although it had stopped raining earlier, more was predicted. "I don't think he's hunting for shells, and it's not exactly prime weather for taking a midnight stroll on the dunes."

Aidan glanced at her, and she could see her own thoughts mirrored in his eyes.

He got up, pulled her out of the hidden room, and went to the closet. He brought out two windbreakers, tossing one to her. His phone and a tiny flashlight went in a pocket and his gun into a shoulder holster.

As he pulled on his own windbreaker, he motioned at the door. "Let's go."

SEVEN

Dirty tricks; aka, covert sabotage

THEY STOLE THROUGH THE NIGHT, partners once more, and Aidan ignored the feeling in his gut warning him this was a bad idea.

Chardy might be out for some fresh air, even though the fog blanketed the beach and dark waters beyond. Bree hurried beside him, barefoot, her watch GPS offering just enough light for Aidan to see part of her face under the hood.

She stayed silent and motioned to the left. Before she stepped off the patio into the sand, he grabbed her hand and put his lips close to her ear. "We stick together, no matter what. If we get separated, you come back here. You don't keep following him or try to intervene in whatever he's about to do, understand?"

He hated to draw a firm boundary, but it had to be done. If

she blew this mission, he might never get another chance to make the Russians pay for what they'd done, and their spy ring would survive and go on to create more problems than he suspected they already had. Boris would live another day, and God only knew what that torturing son-of-a-bitch would do to someone else. *Had* already done.

A curt nod was her only response. He kept hold of her and pulled her behind him.

"Do you miss it?" she murmured. "The excitement and intrigue?"

He was barefoot as well, forgoing shoes in his haste to follow the French double agent. The wet sand felt cold; the fog so heavy it lay like mist on his face. Chardy had to know all the exits were under surveillance, but perhaps he hadn't cared, either because this was a completely innocent walk on a rainy night on the beach, or he assumed he could pass it off as that. If anyone noticed him leaving, particularly Aidan, he could brush it off as nothing more.

"Sometimes. I miss...feeling like I'm helping my country."

She nodded, understanding.

The takedown wasn't until tomorrow night, planned to occur just over the border. The man they were after, leader Boris Vaslov, was coming in on a special transport with non-official cover, and was to be handed off to Chardy. Chardy had been working with several "transporters" as they were called, scouting for Vaslov who held a key role in the spy ring planted throughout Southern Texas and into New Mexico.

It's what the spy master did—excelled at planting Russians so deeply into the US, no one would ever know they were spies. Hiding in plain sight. They could be your doctor, the clerk at the supermarket, your next door neighbor. Some had been planted young, growing up like any middle-class kid in America, but with one very different purpose—if activated by Vaslov, they had a mission. Could be something as low level as hacking into a database to retrieve information. Or as extreme as setting off a bomb or assassinating a high-profile target like a senator, even the president.

This particular ring consisted of a dozen or so trained Russian operatives pretending to be good ol' Southern boys and girls. Behind the scenes, they plotted subversion against the US government and tried to find ways for Russia to sabotage certain banks, cripple oil production, and gain new intelligence sources, none of whom realized they were being targeted.

Their favorites ranged from young, female college students to biker gangs and homegrown survivalists with a bone to chew against the government.

Aidan had managed to find ties to three of the suspected five who had carefully embedded themselves in the area. They needed Vaslov to uncover the final two.

Subversion was a manpower-intensive strategy, and in this case, often took years, decades, to see results. This spy ring was a spin-off of one he and Bree had tried to expose on their last mission together, and by God, he'd make sure they went down in flames this time. He would not allow them to disappear into the American woodwork in order to resurface somewhere else.

The mist turned to rain, and Aidan put up his hood. The windbreaker Bree wore hung almost to her knees, and she had to take two steps for every one of his. Since she had the GPS, he tried to slow down in order for her to take the lead, but she was as anxious as him to keep on Chardy's trail, practically running in her haste and kicking sand on him as she tugged on his hand.

They needed a flashlight, but that would give them away. Aidan hoped the tiny light from Bree's watch wouldn't do the same. The fog was thick enough, he doubted anyone could see it.

Luckily, his internal sense of direction helped guide them away from the waves crashing onto the shore. As they walked north on the beach, lights from various shops also helped, though the fog dampened their illumination considerably.

Bree's hand was chilled and he rubbed his thumb over it, instinctively trying to warm it. She was probably freezing in nothing but the dress and windbreaker, her bare lower legs and feet now soaked. His own pant legs were wet as well, but he had more body mass and natural heat.

He guessed they were a hundred yards north of the spa when she pulled up short. The red dot on her little map had stopped moving north and turned west.

"What do you think he's doing?" she asked quietly.

"Getting wet, that's for sure." Maybe the man had decided to go up the dune and hit one of the boardwalks to the main road lined with condominiums and restaurants. Through the darkness, he could see most of the shops were closed, their windows dark, but a high-rise nearby sprinkled the night sky with dim lights. Down the block, the Russian Orthodox Church stood silent, no decorations as they celebrated the birth of Christ in January, contrasting with the island's florist, whose flashing window displays lit up the area with cheer.

Was Chardy meeting someone at their condo? Was he just looking for a restaurant?

Aidan wanted to believe it was as simple as that, but his gut told him differently.

"He stopped," Bree said, material swishing as she pointed. "Twenty yards or so over there."

They jogged in that direction and came to a set of wooden steps. Sand caked on his feet, he took the stairs two at a time ahead of Bree. On the wind, he thought he heard voices, but with the waves crashing behind him, he couldn't be sure. He put out a hand to stop her. "Stay here."

"No." She slapped his hand away. "I'm going with you."

It was on the tip of his tongue to remind her this could be dangerous, but she lived for danger. The warning would only make her more eager to follow.

He returned his hand to her arm and held it firmly. "Stay behind me and if I tell you to get out of sight, you better do it."

He could see her teeth as she smiled in the shadows. "Or what? You'll hogtie me and throw me over the boardwalk railing?"

The lightheartedness of her tone spoke of her excitement. She thrived on this shit. He couldn't imagine her ever sitting at a desk, like her Uncle Martin, and running the spa. She'd go crazy from the day to day management and customer service. She loved adventure and danger as much as she did her sexy dresses and high heels, more so.

"If he's meeting another involved in this sting operation, I don't want to blow his cover." And if it was someone who'd been involved in the Russian catastrophe, they might recognize him or Bree. So while she lived for danger, Aidan was determined to keep her far away from it.

"We're just a husband and wife out for a walk on the beach." She patted his hand, still on her arm. "Now get a move on before we miss—"

A cry rent the air. For half a second they both froze, then broke into a run.

The planks of the boardwalk were wet and slippery. Aidan could feel the thud of Bree's footsteps behind him. No one was out, thanks to the weather, and as they neared the opposite end, more lights cut through the fog.

A silhouette was bent over a dark mass lying on the ground.

Aidan reached for his gun. The figure rose, face in shadow under the hood of a jacket, and took off running.

A few more strides and he saw the mass on the ground was a man—and dammit, he recognized Chardy.

The blood pouring from a wound on his head looked black in the murky light. Aidan gave thought to pursuing the man running away as Bree fell to her knees to check on Etienne. A low groan came from him and Bree made soothing noises. "Don't move. We'll get help."

Aidan knelt beside the man. "Who was it? Who is your attacker?"

Chardy's eyes rolled up and his body tensed. His head lolled back and forth several times, and Aidan couldn't be sure if he was purposely shaking it no or was, indeed, having a seizure brought on by the head wound.

Bree tapped at her watch face, dialing for help, and as the 911 call went through, she ripped a piece of fabric from the bottom of her dress. She reeled off their approximate location to the operator. "A man has been seriously injured. We need an ambulance immediately."

Chardy grabbed her arm and tried to say something. Aidan took the fabric from her and wadded it up to hold against the wound. "I'm...sorry," he said through gritted teeth.

The man was apologizing for betraying her as if...

He thought he was going to die.

She held still for a moment, staring at him. "When you're back on your feet, I'll punch you in the nose for what you did to Aidan and I, and we'll call it even, okay? Now tell me who the hell did this to you."

He released is grip, his shaking hand going to his neck. And then, *shit*, white foam started coming out of the corner of his mouth, his body spasming once more.

Bree's eyes snapped up to Aidan's. "Poison?"

Aidan yanked Chardy's hand from his neck, his arm falling limply to his side. In the gloom, he couldn't be sure but he thought he saw something. Snagging his flashlight from his pocket, he shone it on Chardy's neck and saw a ghostly drop of blood from a tiny puncture wound.

The attacker had not only whacked Chardy on the head, he'd injected him with something lethal.

Chardy gasped for air, arching off the ground, eyes rolling up once more. Without knowing what type of poison, Aidan had no idea how to counteract it before the ambulance arrived.

"Etienne!" He grabbed him by the shoulders, trying to help him weather the spasms. "Who did this to you?"

The man's mouth moved, and only incoherent sounds came out of it. Bree leaned her ear down to his mouth. More sounds that made no sense to Aidan. There was no way to save him; whatever the poison was, it was acting fast.

Gurgling, more foam coming from his mouth, Chardy nevertheless tried to form words. "Ma...mar..."

Bree frowned, shifting her gaze to Aidan. He shook his head.

"Ttt..."

Another hard convulsion and his body went limp.

"Shit." Aidan motioned Bree back and began chest compressions. In the distance, he heard the sirens.

They did their best to keep Chardy alive, but by the time the EMTs arrived, the spy had long since lost a pulse. As Aidan and Bree moved so the medics could work on him, Bree threaded her fingers through Aidan's.

"What kind of poison?" A female EMT called to them.

"No idea," Aidan responded, "but we think it was injected in his neck from what he was able to convey when we found him."

As she administered some type of medicine, her partner charged a defibrillator. Aidan and Bree watched them work on restarting his heart and counteracting the poison.

For several tense moments, Aidan was sure Chardy was dead. Drawn by the sirens and lights, people began crowding around, despite the rain that was now falling again. A police cruiser arrived and two officers jumped out, one moving the crowd back, while the second approached the scene.

Aidan squeezed Bree's hand. "Let me handle this."

For once, she didn't argue, and Aidan kept his description to the cop brief. Like Bree had suggested, he told the officer the two of them were out for a walk, heard a cry, and stumbled across the attack. No, they hadn't seen the attacker, and Aidan explained that Etienne Chardy was a guest at the spa where he worked.

By the time he and Bree finished giving their statements, the EMTs were loading Chardy into the back of the ambulance. An oxygen mask was over his mouth.

"Is he alive?" Bree called to the female medic.

"Barely." She nodded at the two of them. "Good work. If it hadn't been for you, he wouldn't be breathing right now."

"You think he'll make it?" Aidan asked.

Her face said no as she climbed in, but she was a professional. "We'll do everything we can for him."

The crowd began to drift off and the officer they'd spoken to passed by with a warning. "We'll be in touch if we have other questions. Don't leave town."

Bree's face was a mask as they stood and watched it pull away. "Now what?"

He didn't need to ask what she was referring to. Chardy was his way in with the Russian spy ring. He was the transporter to pick up Vaslov. Bree didn't even know that part—that Vaslov was within spitting distance if the intel was accurate. Without Chardy, Aidan would never uncover the names and identities of the others.

Aidan needed to be sure Chardy was under security at the

hospital. Whoever had done this might've been watching and realized he'd failed. At least, for the moment.

Most likely, the double agent would die, but the killer couldn't be sure he hadn't shared a name or some identifying information.

"Let's get back to the spa," he told her, scanning what was left of the crowd. "It's going to be a long night."

The rain pelted down on them as they turned to retrace their footsteps. They were silent the whole time, Joey meeting them at the door.

"What the hell happened?" he asked, holding the door as they came in. "I heard it on the scanner."

Aidan gave him the watered down version he'd told the cop. Joey narrowed his eyes, as if he didn't quite believe it, then he nodded. "That sucks, man. The guy was kind of a ball buster, but what a horrible way to go. Who would do that to him?"

Aidan shrugged, wishing he knew. He and Bree were both soaking wet, still barefoot, and had a lot to discuss. The night clerk behind the desk offered to bring them towels from the back room, but Aidan waved her off. He drew Bree away from Joey, toward the elevators. "If the police come by to check his room notify me immediately. No one goes in their without me."

Another nod. "You got it, boss."

Before they made it to the elevators, Bree took his hand and changed their direction.

"Where are we going?"

Her face was drawn, eyes hard. "To see my uncle."

"Don't you want to cleanup first? Get out of those wet clothes?"

"No," she said. "What I want to know is why he just tried to kill one of our guests."

WILDERNESS OF MIRRORS

BREE STOOD outside Uncle Martin's door, feeling slightly ashamed of herself.

"You really think he had something to do with this?" Aidan asked beside her. "You can't be serious."

God she felt horrible. But she would feel worse if Martin was actually involved. Who else knew about Aidan's assignment? "I couldn't make out for sure what Chardy said, but the syllables... I could put together as 'Martin."

Aidan shook his head, fingers rubbing tired eyes. "Why would he kill...?"

The door swung open and Uncle Martin stood there with Princess Gracie in one arm. He looked them over from head to toe, the sight of their wet hair, Bree's torn dress, and their dirty feet made his eyebrows rise. "What the hell happened to you two?"

"Can we come in?" Bree asked.

He swept back and motioned them in. His suite on the third floor faced west over the island and was half the size of the penthouse. It was decorated like it was on the Caribbean coast rather than the Texan one with flamboyant colors and a unique style that matched the man himself.

He was dressed in a turquoise and black pajama outfit with a matching robe. His feet were in slippers, and Princess Gracie wore a nightgown in the same colors.

"Did you happen to go for a walk on the beach tonight?" Bree questioned him. She noticed his hair was dry, the chihuahua's long, black and white fur was as well.

"Yes." He glanced between her and Aidan. "Are you two okay?"

Aidan crossed his arms over his chest. "Why?"

"I took Gracie for her evening constitutional, like I always do."

"In the rain?" Bree responded.

"We both wore our raincoats. What's going on?"

"Did you meet any of our guests while you were on your walk?" Aidan asked, sounding every bit the interrogator.

Martin took a step back and looked both of them over again, the wheels in his head turning. "What is this? Are you two questioning me for a reason?"

That sick feeling in Bree's stomach returned. "Etienne Chardy was attacked on the boardwalk half a mile north of here. Someone hit him over the back of the head, and once he was incapacitated, they injected poison into his system."

Martin's face deflated. He hugged Gracie a little tighter and walked to his recliner, dropping into it and rubbing a hand over his face. The recliner was a cherry red color, clashing with his ensemble. Bree sat across from him on the edge of the couch leaning onto her elbows. "Did Aidan tell you who this man really is?"

Martin shot a look at her. "Yes, and if he's dead, I won't cry over it. He betrayed you and Aidan and nearly got you both killed. In my book, he deserves whatever he got."

"Uncle Martin—"

He held up a hand to stop her. "I can't believe you'd even think so poorly of me. Are you actually accusing me of doing such a thing?"

She couldn't quite believe she was either. "He was able to get out a couple syllables before he become unconscious," she told him. "They could combine to make the first part of your name. That's the only reason I'm asking if you had anything to do with this."

His brows rose higher than she'd ever seen them go, and he looked as if she'd slapped him. "Why would I kill the man, other than for revenge, which you would then kick my ass for?"

On the TV, the holiday classic, *White Christmas* played, and in the back of her mind, Bree remembered it was her mother's favorite. The queasy stomach paled in comparison to the pain in her heart at seeing the actors on screen and remembering her mom singing along with them.

Blinking away tears, she refocused on her uncle. "You knew Aidan was running an undercover sting with Chardy, right?"

Uncle Martin waved a hand around. "I didn't know the details, and I don't want to. Aidan said it had something to do with taking out the leader of the spy ring the two of you were after when all that awful stuff went down in Russia. That's all I needed to know. I swear to you I had nothing to do with what happened to that double crossing piece of crap."

The *leader* of the spy ring? Wait... Aidan hadn't said anything about that.

Bree looked at her husband, saw the tense stance and studious eyes, his insightful stare sizing up her uncle. "This has to do with Vaslov?"

Aidan only nodded, jaw clenched.

For half a second, she couldn't think, couldn't breathe. This put a whole new spin on things, and once again, she felt a horrible disheartenment that Aidan hadn't told her the whole truth.

"I have to call this in," Aidan said, heading for the door.

"Is he dead?" Uncle Martin asked. Princess Gracie wasn't sure if Martin was upset or ready to relax. She turned circles in his lap, eyeing him, jumping at his chest.

The poor dog was as confused as Bree. "We thought we lost

him, but Aidan did CPR, and resuscitated him until the EMTs arrived. They were taking him to the hospital, but we doubt he'll make it through the night."

"I'll keep you posted, sir," Aidan said over his shoulder as he walked out.

Bree stood and gave her uncle an apologetic smile. "I'm sorry for the accusation. Just trying to get my bearings with all of this."

He sniffed, as much a diva as Gracie. "I suppose I'll let you make it up to me in the morning."

She had no idea for sure what he was going to require, but she knew it would be a doozy.

She caught up with Aidan at the elevator, riding to the fourth floor in silence. Hoping he had a good reason for not telling her about Vaslov—well, she knew why he'd kept that piece of the puzzle to himself. *To protect me.*

It always came back to that. She wanted to be mad, but found she didn't have it in her. Lately, she wondered if she did, indeed, need protection. From herself as much as anyone else.

They stood in front of Chardy's room, Aidan using his keycard to access it.

"I thought you had to call your handler, or whoever's in charge of this sting operation."

"I do." He opened the door and walked in. "But I figured you might want to remove anything you put in here before the detectives show to look at the man's personal belongings.

Good thinking. She was also going to grab Chardy's laptop. "I didn't get to check the safe," she said. "Can you get into it?"

Aidan rolled his eyes, as if it were child's play, then pulled his cell from his back pocket and started texting.

Bree had planted three listening devices, so she went to the various rooms collecting them. She brushed her stringy wet hair out of her face and looked for the laptop. When she'd been here earlier, it had sat on the desk in the far corner, but now it was empty except for a landline.

She started to follow Aidan to the cabinet where the safe was to see if it was in there, but his phone rang, and when he looked at the caller ID, he said, "I need to take this."

He strode across the room and went onto the balcony, closing the patio door behind him securely and giving her a look that told her in no uncertain terms she was not to eavesdrop.

Of course, that's exactly what she planned to do.

She had to be subtle, so she continued searching for a moment where he could see her before she disappeared into the bedroom. Since she didn't see the laptop in there either, she went to the matching balcony door across from the bed and stayed behind the curtain, pressing her ear as close to the glass as she could in hopes of overhearing what Aidan was saying to his handler.

His voice was low, as if he suspected she was close by, but mostly all he said were details about what had happened to Chardy, and that, no, he had no idea who'd done it.

"I'm screwed with this operation," she heard him say. "I can't take Chardy's place, because Vaslov will recognize me."

The meetup with Vaslov was less than twenty-four hours from now. The Russian spy ring leader would be suspicious of anyone taking his place, and Bree mentally cursed that she couldn't do it, but he knew her, having doled out some nasty torture on her, and he definitely knew Aidan.

Once again, her stomach fell, realizing this might have been their last chance to finally put him out of commission and shut him down.

By the time Aidan disconnected, she had hustled back to where the safe was. He gave her a look suggesting he knew she hadn't been standing there the whole time, but he said nothing.

Aidan punched in a number and spoke when someone on the other end answered. "I'm going to need to see the video footage of everyone who left the spa between six and seven tonight, Joey." There was a pause. "Yeah, I'll be there in a few minutes. Appreciate it, man."

He ended the call and bent to enter the code on the keypad. A moment later it opened. "All the safes are programmed with a digital override, just in case."

"And here I thought you knew everyone's personal combination," she said.

He didn't appreciate her flippancy, and swung the door wider. Bree looked over his shoulder to see inside and her brows crashed down. "What the hell?" she said under her breath.

Aidan began pulling out the contents, including the laptop, as well as a medical kit. He unzipped it, his gaze coming up to hers. Apparently, she wasn't the only one confused at the syringes and several bottles of some kind of injectable solution.

Aidan pulled out a vial. There was no label. "What do you think he was doing with this?"

Bree's head spun. She looked between the syringes and bottle, then back, thinking about the needle puncture in Chardy's neck. "Oh my god," she said. "Aidan, I don't think whoever he was meeting planned to kill him. I think it was just the opposite."

A muscle jumped in Aidan's jaw. He dropped the vial into the medical kit and sighed heavily. His phone rang and he answered, his eyes locking on hers as he received information. "Yeah, okay. Thanks for letting us know."

He finished then tapped it against his leg. "Chardy's dead."

Her heart sank, even though it wasn't surprising. "Whoever he was meeting tonight, *he* planned to kill *them*." She chewed on her bottom lip, trying to imagine what Chardy had been up to. "He had the poison, but somehow ended up being injected by his own syringe."

"A couple detectives are on their way to examine his belongings and question us further." Aidan closed the safe. "We better get cleaned up and see what's on this laptop."

Bree followed him out and paused in the hallway. He took her to the penthouse and dropped her at her front door. "Meet me downstairs at the security office as soon as you can," he said.

She was exhausted, and starving. Now they had to spend another hour or two talking to the cops and trying to figure out what they were going to do tomorrow night. At least, she hoped, Aidan would let her help.

As he started to walk away, she grabbed him by the hand and pulled him toward her. "I'm going to help you. Don't give up on the mission yet. We'll figure something out."

He looked into her eyes and she felt something stir deep in her belly. He moved a strand of wet hair from her face before he tipped his head down and brushed a kiss across her lips. "Thank you," he murmured.

Then he was gone.

EIGHT

T_aking command of the target_

AIDAN SAT AT HIS DESK, his eyes sandpaper, a twitch in his neck muscles. The adrenaline was long gone, exhaustion engulfing him like a blanket. Four a.m., another long night.

After he and Bree had spoken to the detectives, reviewed security footage in and around the spa, they'd attempted to hack into the encrypted files on the laptop. They had been unsuccessful with that, and Bree had called one of the people in her organization – Shadow Force International – and had some guy named Rory working on breaking it.

Aidan wasn't optimistic. The CIA's abilities surpassed anyone's he'd ever encountered.

What the hell had Chardy been doing, meeting someone on that boardwalk? Why did he have what they assumed to be a poisonous substance and syringes? Aidan had hoped the cameras might show the man exiting the spa with someone, or perhaps meeting them in the parking lot before they went for the walk, but there had been nothing. Footage from inside had shown nothing more than Chardy leaving his room, going downstairs, and speaking briefly with Megan as she was on her way home after her day. She'd headed to the parking lot, while Chardy went in the opposite direction toward the beach. No one else had interacted with him before he left, and Aidan couldn't speak to Megan until her shift started at eight.

His mission was over, and damn it, he'd been so close to shutting down the espionage ring that'd gotten away from him, to capturing the man who tortured and nearly killed Bree.

It was all he had lived for since she had sent him away.

His gaze wandered to his bed where she rested on top of the covers. After hours of combing through footage and the laptop, and finding nothing, she'd fallen asleep at the table. Aidan had carried her to his bed, where she was now completely zonked.

Sitting back in his chair, Aidan rubbed his eyes and blew out a disgusted breath. His handler was furious about Chardy and the blown mission. The CIA had been tracking Boris Vaslov for years, and if he got wind of what happened to Chardy...he'd never surface again.

Debating whether to make a fresh pot of coffee and stay up, or try to catnap before his day began, Aidan watched Bree. She'd exchanged the wet torn dress for a pair of sweatpants and a t-shirt, her hair in a messy braid , multiple strands teased out of it and spread across his pillow.

It'd been two years since he'd seen her like this, in his bed, and the emotions that swept over him were as thick as the exhaustion. It had taken a goatfuck of a situation to land her there, and he wasn't sorry about that, but there was no way he could salvage the assignment now, and his marriage was still on the rocks.

Maybe he should take her up on her offer and work for the organization she did. Perhaps he could salvage their marriage and prove the extent to which he'd go to have her back in his life.

Rising slowly, he stretched, never taking his eyes off her. He'd go to any lengths to save her, protect her, love her. She'd made it clear she didn't want any of that from him, but it was in his blood, his very cells.

He would never give up on her, on the love he felt for her. He took their marriage vows seriously, and he'd be damned if he didn't spend every moment from here on out romancing his wife back into a loving relationship.

She would never be safe if Vaslov was running around, no matter who she worked for and how extensive their security measures were. Even if he had to become a shadow in the dark, and never let her know he was watching out for her, that's exactly what he would do.

She shifted, curling in a ball, and he realized she was probably chilled. He found a blanket and drew it over her.

She stirred, eyes blinking open, and grabbed his hand just as he was about to walk away. "What time is it?" she asked.

"Just after four."

She tugged, pulling him down. "Come to bed."

Her insistent hand, her sleepy voice, the exhaustion flooding through him... It was too much to resist.

Everything below his waist stirred to life, even though the rest of his body screamed for slumber. Lying beside her was dangerous. No telling what could happen, especially if he did fall asleep and end up in the nightmare.

After Russia they'd both suffered from them, but Bree seemed to have moved on from hers. He wasn't sure he'd ever be able to. Having her so close while he slept was dangerous in and of itself. He couldn't control his desire for her. Nor the longing, the ache, she always brought out in him. Since that first night in Vegas, she'd been the need he could never satisfy.

"Aidan," she said, "you've got to rest. I won't leave until we figure this out." She patted the comforter. "I mean it, come to bed."

The arguments in his head drifted away at the sound of her voice. Against his better judgment, he slid in, lying on his back and closing his eyes.

He made sure not to touch her, but it did no good. She rolled over and tucked herself against him, using the blanket to cover them as she laid her head on his shoulder. Within seconds, her breathing deepened once again and he knew she was out.

He followed her down into the depths of sleep, his dreams filled with her. She was laughing and teasing him, running from him through a park with green grass and tall trees. Sunlight glinted off her copper hair as it blew behind her. She shot him a look over her shoulder and waved him on to follow her, so he did.

But in the next instant, he was inside that black prison again. Her laughter turned to screams, echoing off the walls, vibrating through his body and into his bones. He tried to yell, call her name, but his voice was locked inside his throat.

He couldn't move, shackles around his wrists and ankles. The vise grip was back around his chest, crushing him. He forced his voice out from the lockdown of his throat. "Bree!" he screamed. "I'm coming for you. I'm coming!"

"Aidan," he heard a voice say close to his ear. He struggled against the shackles, his helplessness and inability to get to her.

"Aidan!"

He sat straight up, eyes blinking, but what he saw was the

prison walls, the concrete floor. Hands touched his shoulder, his back. He jumped.

"Aidan, it's me, Bree."

He snapped into the present, and found her beside him. Everything came tumbling back, a chain link, bit by bit falling in to place.

"The nightmares again?" Her voice was soft, the hands rubbing him gentle, as if he were a child waking from a night terror.

He leaned forward setting his elbows on his bent knees and dropped his face into his hands. "Jesus, I'm sorry."

She hugged him. "Don't worry about it. Stress can bring on the nightmares. You've had an enormous amount of it in the past twenty-four hours."

He blew out a sigh and looked at her. "Do you still get them after a stressful day?"

She nodded once. "Not as much as I used to, but sometimes shit just happens."

Bree had always had a way of blowing things off, serious situations like trauma and death, and moving on. The only thing she never had was the death of her mother.

She leaned her head onto his shoulder, keeping her gaze on his. "I'm sorry about your mission. I really am."

She was so close he could smell her shampoo. Her hands felt like brands burning right through his shirt into his skin. Before his brain could fully return online, he found himself turning toward her, gripping the back of her neck and pulling her so their lips were almost touching. "My god, I've missed you so much."

She knew how to soothe the demons he fought day and night. She always had. It was what had attracted him in Vegas. Sure, he'd been there for a weekend of fun, but it had felt kind of hollow. He and some of his SEAL brothers had had leave and were looking for a good time. His showed up in Bree Russo, the fiery, spunky woman who dressed all in black, and wasn't the least interested in him until she'd had several rounds of drinks.

Her lips parted slightly as if she were about to respond, but she didn't say anything, her eyes scanning, searching his as if she were gazing into his soul. She'd always been able to do that, mesmerizing him with silence and those uncanny looks.

"How did I ever get so lucky to find you?" he asked softly.

In the next moment, her lips moved just enough to brush his. "I'm not sure I'd call it lucky."

He knew what she meant. She'd always believed she was damaged goods. He knew better, and he'd tried over and over to make her understand how incredible she was.

It was in that moment, nose to nose, their eyes locked, that he knew he would accept the position with Shadow Force International without a doubt. Not just because his mission was blown, or Bree had asked, but she always knew how to throw him a lifeline, and every time he accepted, it changed his life for the better. Even their screwed up, wacky marriage was more than he could have ever imagined for himself when he left the Navy. She was his true north, and no matter what chaos their marriage entailed, he was in one hundred percent.

The hand on his back moved slowly up his shoulders to the base of his neck, into his hair. She massaged the area, trailing her fingers to his ear and running one around the edge, all the way down to the lobe. From there she traced his jaw to the front until their faces kept her from going farther. The finger went to his lips and touched them gently as well. "I've missed you too."

She spoke so softly he almost didn't hear her, but then he was kissing her, words no longer important. Their bodies came together and melted as easily as their lips found each other.

He wanted to slow things down, relish the moment of having her back in his arms, in his bed, but Bree seemed to have a different agenda. She broke the kiss, shoving him slightly so she could help get his shirt over his head. She shucked it to the floor, kissed him frantically again, then broke away to shed her own.

Another kiss, then she went up on her knees, pushing her sweatpants down. She kissed him as she wiggled out of them, doing a dance that would make an acrobat jealous.

He removed his just as quickly between kisses and soon they were naked, falling on the bed again, reveling in each other's bodies.

He trailed kisses down her neck, her collarbone, down to her breasts, even as he caressed her thighs, her hips and up to her belly. She moaned and arched into his hands, his lips.

Everything in him was taut with need. His heart thundered in his chest, his body and soul filled with delicious desire and happiness.

Her eyes closed, her body moving under him, and he couldn't get enough of her. He licked and kissed, bit and sucked, loving all the reactions he got from her. She slid her hands over the hardness of him, grinding herself into him, and scratching her nails down his back.

"I need to touch you," she moaned.

He needed to touch her too, to believe this was real. So he did.

He went over her inch by inch, exploring what he'd missed for two years. It was almost like their first time, and he was damn well gonna make the best of it.

When they finally came together, he slipped inside her and nearly lost himself. The sensation was so familiar and yet it had been such a long dry spell, he nearly lost control and went over the edge. Bree bit his earlobe, nipped at his neck, and he had to draw back for a moment, lifting his chest off hers, pulling his mouth from her warm heated skin.

He searched her eyes, took in her beauty and promised himself he would never stay away from her again, no matter how much she ordered or begged. This is where she belonged, with him, and he would do what he had to do to prove it to her. As he thrust into her deeply again, and began to build a rhythm for them, he saw the promise in her eyes.

It surprised him, that look, and he wondered if it was just the sex speaking for her, or if she had possibly changed her mind about moving forward with their marriage.

But his body was in control at the moment, and whatever promises and secrets lay in the depths of her eyes, he would have to explore later.

***

ONCE IS AN ACCIDENT. *Twice is a coincidence. Three times is enemy action.*

BREE'S PHONE rang on the nightstand, waking her from a sound sleep. Without opening her eyes, she reached for it, her other hand on a warm, firm, muscled chest. Even with everything going on, she felt a sense of peace. Her sleep, what little she'd had, had been amazing.

Her body wanted to stay right there, snuggled in bed with Aidan, so she brought the phone to her lips and answered, "Hello?"

Rory was on the other end. "Hello, cupcake. Sleeping in today?"

Sighing, she swung her legs around and sat up. "No rest for the wicked. You know that, Rory."

He chatted for a moment regarding info he'd uncovered about Etienne Chardy and his bona fides. The bastard had turned double agent yet again.

Disgusted, Bree wondered who he'd really worked for, certainly not his own country, Russia, or the United States. It appeared it was only for himself and the fallout could be enormous.

"I broke through some of the encryption," Rory said. "Chardy offered intel about two Russians inside the consulate working for the United States to the highest bidder. There are multiple encrypted messages to a bidder called Apple Pie Mama. I traced that to one of the suspected members of the spy ring McNamara is going after."

"Two Russians inside the consulate who are giving up information to the CIA?" Bree shook her head. "And Chardy was selling their names in exchange for what?"

"Three billion dollars. Apparently, he was meeting Vaslov to deliver them. He was poisoned with a liquid nerve agent favored by Russian spies, so you put the pieces together."

Bree sighed heavily and glanced at Aidan. He was awake and his intense stare made her shiver. "Was he double crossing Aidan?" she asked.

"Looks like he was working both sides pretty well," Rory said. "He was giving up the consulate Russians for the money and Vaslov to McNamara."

"Covering all his bases then. He wanted Vaslov out of the game just in case, didn't he?"

"Appears so," Rory confirmed.

Aidan laid a hand on her arm, his brows rising with questions. She would fill him in in a minute. "Book me on the first flight back to D.C.," she told Rory.

Before he could answer, Beatrice popped on the line "Have you completed your mission, Hathor?"

Had she been on speakerphone all this time? "No, but —"

"Your orders stand. I will alert the Russians at the consulate in question about possible compromise. I'll take care of things on this end; you do the same there."

Bree started to argue, then realized Beatrice had the resources to do exactly that and there was no real reason for her to return yet. Still, she felt like Beatrice was taking this out of her hands, and then, following that thought, she realized it had never really been in them.

This had been Aidan's mission, not hers. She had nothing to stand on in order to argue, and since she was already in the doghouse with Beatrice, it was best to tuck her tail and do as told.

Not her style at all. But truly, what could she gain by refusing to cooperate?

"Your service is greatly appreciated," Beatrice said. "You and Mr. McNamara did a good job. Your nation will be grateful. Now complete your assignment."

The line went dead. Bree dropped the phone into her lap and scrubbed her face with her hands.

Aidan grabbed her wrist and forced her to look at him. "What did he say?"

Damn, she wished she could crawl back into bed with him. Feel him wrap his arms around her and make the world go away for a few more hours.

"Etienne was playing the US and the Russians." She explained everything Rory had told her, watching Aidan's face fall.

She hated seeing that expression, the slump of his shoulders, as he moved to stand. He'd held out hope there was some way they could salvage this.

She'd wanted nothing more, had hoped Rory would be able to come up with something that would provide closure.

Taking down Vaslov would have been the ultimate end to Aidan's relationship with the CIA. It would have given both of them some peace, but now, they had nothing. Boris was still running loose, and surely he'd heard about Chardy, if he wasn't behind it himself. There was nothing they could do at this point.

Bree stood and slid her arms around his neck. "We'll get him," she promised. "If it's the last thing I ever do, I will make sure we stop him."

Aidan leaned his forehead against hers, his hands going around her waist and tugging her closer. "I was doing it for you, you know. That bastard doesn't deserve to walk the earth, and I wanted to end him. I wanted my face to be the last thing he saw before he died, so he would know what he did to you was the reason I came after him."

There was nothing else to say, nothing else to do. Bree went up on her toes and kissed him.

Uncle Martin was counting on her to help with the Winter Lights Hop, and Bree was determined not to let him down. Since she wouldn't be returning to D.C. just yet – she hadn't had a chance to confirm with Aidan he'd leave his position here and go with her – she still had a commitment to her uncle.

She handed out assignments, and extra staff filtered through the lobby, kitchen, and the spa areas that would be on display for the open house. Thank god for Megan, her uncle's assistant. She was one of the most organized people Bree had ever met, and she understood how much Uncle Martin depended on her.

Both front desk clerks were in attendance to book appointments for anyone who wanted to schedule a massage, facial, etc. Chef Condor had made additional Christmas cookies and pretty little tarts, and there was punch, eggnog, and hot chocolate.

Everything was decorated beautifully, and Bree felt a pang of sadness that her mother wasn't there to see it. The holidays had always been her favorite time of year, and she'd reveled in making the Gulf Breeze the most beautiful place around. It was like a fantasy land, and seeing all the decorations her mother had once used made Bree's heart both happy and nostalgic.

Her emotions were all muddled about Aidan too. She was excited and apprehensive about this new dynamic. She'd spent the last two years trying to convince herself, and him, they had no future, and yet here she was, doing just the opposite of what she'd planned.

She'd fallen in love with him all over again, damn it. She'd never expected a reconciliation. If she got Aidan to join Shadow Force and go to DC, she'd intended to stay and help Uncle Martin. Joey was the most likely person to step in to Aidan's shoes and take over security, but Uncle Martin would be upset to lose Aidan. He was such an integral part of the spa now.

She and Aidan had made love again in his room, then slept a few more hours and rose just before noon. Because of the open house, they hadn't had much time to talk, both needing to clean up and get ready. She'd come downstairs dressed in a red sparkling skirt and blouse and was looking for Aidan, when Joey went hustling past her. "Joey, have you seen Aidan?"

"Uhh, he went to run an errand, probably for your uncle. Sorry, I just got here—had to help Mrs. Hiyak with a keycard malfunction, and hold her hand for a while. She's needy— scared about her security—after the Chardy incident, you know." Joey glanced at his watch. "He texted and said he'd be back before it officially starts, so it should be any minute now."

She felt slightly peeved neither Aidan nor her uncle had mentioned it to her, but why would they? She wasn't part of the hotel's "team" in reality, and before she could text Aidan, she was swept up in a conversation with one of the guests.

Promptly at three o'clock, Megan opened the front doors and a stream of people flooded in, many dressed in holiday attire, and all of them *oohing* and *ahhing* over the decorations, the spread of food in the dining room, and filing through to take a tour of the spa service area.

Uncle Martin and Princess Gracie were the hosts, both immensely enjoying being the center of attention. Uncle Martin lead the tours and snuck cookies for himself and the dog as he went.

When there was no sign of Aidan after another hour, Bree purposely searched out her uncle and drew him aside from a conversation with two women, one being Loretta, the florist.

"Have you seen Aidan?" he asked. "Joey said he was running an errand for you and was supposed to back by now. I can't find him."

Anxiety was eating at her stomach, and while she wanted to enjoy the cookies and hot chocolate, she had no appetite.

"He told me one of the security cameras was down and needed a part from town, so he was picking that up," Martin said.

Bree felt her stomach drop. She took off for the elevator, Uncle Martin calling behind her, "Is everything okay?"

Everything was definitely not okay. Where had Aidan gone? Surely, he wasn't still trying to make that meet with Vaslov? There was no way. Even if Boris showed up, he'd recognize Aidan and try to kill him.

Upstairs in her room, she quickly changed clothes, grabbed

her backpack, and loaded it with several items including her gun. She hustled downstairs and to the parking lot to find her car, not waiting for the valet.

She'd just unlocked it and thrown her backpack in when she felt a blow to the back of her head. Her knees buckled, her body pitching forward.

The sharp edge of the car door slammed in to her temple. Blackness surrounded her before she hit the ground.

NINE

Spies are social people, except when they're not

GOD HE HATED PARTIES. Aidan was almost glad he had to find a replacement for the parking lot camera that had suddenly stopped working. He needed to take a breather, get away for a few minutes, and regroup.

He was fucking happy. No matter the fact his mission was a bust. Bree was his.

He would hunt down Vaslov. He would never stop looking for the bastard. But for now, for tonight, he had what he wanted—his wife back.

On his way across the bridge to the mainland, he considered going after him on his own. The original plan was to follow Chardy that night across the border to meet the spy master and ringleader. Once the man was on American soil, Aidan would've called the FBI, since they had jurisdiction, to arrest him, but not before he took a shot at getting the names of the last two spies embedded in South Texas.

With no one to meet Vaslov, and the strong possibility the man knew what had happened to Chardy, Aidan doubted there was any reason to go tonight. Even if Vaslov showed by some miracle, he'd recognize Aidan and do his best to escape arrest. Since Aidan was working under a non-official cover, he'd be alone in Mexico going after a top Russian spy.

He probably could've done it if he'd had backup, but Bree was the only person available, and that was out of the question. He never wanted her within shouting distance of Vaslov again.

So instead, Aidan went to the only electronics store open on a Saturday night on the mainland, and picked up a temporary replacement.

On his way back, he got stuck in traffic on the bridge, hundreds of people heading to the island for the Winter Lights Hop.

Bree had called twice and left messages. *"Where the hell are you?"*

She'd texted the same, and he'd been struggling whether to answer.

He wanted Vaslov so bad he could taste it, and one of the reasons he hadn't spoken to her before he left was because, in all honesty, he didn't know what he was going to do. Taking off to the border appealed on many levels. Ending this tonight. Taking revenge for what Vaslov had done to Bree. It had scrambled his brain, and yet he was smart enough to know the futility of chasing after the man with no backup, and the possibility Vaslov wouldn't show anyway.

As long as he wasn't moving, he texted a reply to Bree. *"On my way with the new camera. Stuck in traffic, so may be a while."*

He was so damn in love with her it hurt. All he'd wanted to

do for the last couple years was end this nightmare with Vaslov on the loose. The game wasn't over yet, not by a long shot, and Aidan was already considering a host of possibilities for taking the man down along with his compatriots.

Twenty minutes later, he pulled into the Gulf Breeze Spa lot and shut off his vehicle. The lot was almost full, and as he stood across from the building, he noticed Bree's car in the valet parking area, the driver's side open.

He stopped in mid-stride, nerves suddenly on alert. What the hell?

People came and went, cars leaving and new ones replacing them. He scanned the area for Bree but couldn't spot her.

At her car, he found a backpack haphazardly tossed on the floor of the passenger seat, as if she'd thrown it there before sitting down.

Where is she?

Snatching it up, he closed the door and looked around again. She was nowhere to be seen, and his gut crawled with a sense of dread.

Taking the backpack with him, he hustled in to find Joey, but came across Martin first.

"Have you seen Bree?" he asked the man.

Martin was in a circle of friends, smiling and happy. Loretta was laughing at a joke, it seemed. Princess Gracie was in his arms and he barely glanced at Aidan.

Then, seeing Aidan's expression, he did a double take. He moved away and searched Aidan's face. "She was here just a minute ago," he said. "Why do you look so worried?"

"Did she go to her car to get something?"

Martin shook his head and shrugged. "Not that I know of."

Aidan unzipped the backpack and looked at the contents – a set of clothes, a cell phone, a gun and bullets. The thing his gaze snagged on was the biggest – Chardy's laptop. "This was in her car and the driver's door was open. She's nowhere in the parking lot."

Martin shrugged again. "Where would she go? She's been hosting the open house."

Aidan took out his phone and dialed her number, the call going directly to voicemail.

His stomach fell. Holy Jesus was she going after Vaslov?

Joey spotted them and hustled up. "Hey, Wylin just told me the security camera for the parking lot is down. I've been tied up with guests and didn't notice."

"I texted you about it earlier, but guess you were busy." Aidan tossed him the replacement, holding out hope he was wrong. "Have you seen Bree?"

"She was looking for you a minute ago," Joey said. He glanced behind him, scanning the crush of people enjoying themselves. "Wonder where she took off to?"

"Christ." Aidan looked at the camera box, the backpack. His suspicious mind started snapping the pieces of the puzzle together. "Someone kidnapped her."

Both men looked at him in confusion. Martin's voice rose an octave "What?"

"What's going on, boss?" Joey asked. "Why would someone kidnap Bree?"

The kid didn't know about her background, knew nothing about the spy ring or Aidan's involvement with the CIA.

He took off running toward the security room. Joey followed on his heels, Martin behind him. By the time the two burst into the room, Aidan already had Wylen, his night security guard, searching video footage of Bree leaving the building.

Sure enough, they found it, but because of the broken camera, they lost her after she exited the side door.

Aidan punched the countertop. "She never came back in.

Someone grabbed her out there, that's why her door was open. That's why the fucking camera is broken."

"What the hell?" Joey murmured.

Martin looked like he was going to be sick. "Why? Who? Do you think it's the same person that killed Etienne Chardy?"

"Can someone fill me in on what's going on here?" Joey wanted to know.

"Sorry," Aidan said. "Later."

The sheer amount of people coming and going would make it impossible to figure out who might've kidnapped her and where they'd taken here. A roaring anger swept through Aidan – anger at himself as well as the kidnapper.

He called her again, but got the same result and his mind swiftly calculated how long it would take to knock her on the back of the head and stuff her into a car pulled up next to hers. It could happen in the blink of an eye, and the jovial people at the open house would never notice.

He felt as sick as Martin looked.

"Show me the front entrance," he told Wylen. "I want to look at every car that left from the time we lost Bree until five minutes later."

There were five vehicles, more entering than leaving. Only one was from out of town, the rest all had Texas plates, and Aidan felt his heart sink. There was no way to tell who might have taken her. He'd have to track down all five, and as quickly as possible. Time was not on his side; it had already been nearly an hour.

Except...

Scrolling through the contact list on his phone, he found the number Bree had given him for the head of Shadow Force International, Beatrice Reese. He hit the call button, clenched his jaw, and paced as it rang on the other end.

"Mr. McNamara," the woman said in greeting. "What have you done with my operative?"

How did she know something was wrong? "She's been kidnapped," he ground out. "Tell me you have a tracker on her."

There was a charged pause. "You don't?"

"I used to." He smacked the wall. "It was in her wedding band. I'm sure she disposed of it a long time ago."

"One moment, please."

Aidan pulled the phone from his ear and stared at it incredulously. His finger was poised over the disconnect button when she came back on and said, "The GPS tracking is still on and no, I won't tell her. It appears she's approximately three blocks from you at the Russian Orthodox Church."

Fuck. In his mind's eye, he could see Bree's dead body lying on the floor, bleeding out under a cross, or dumped in the graveyard out back. His knees nearly buckled and he swayed at the vision as Beatrice rattled off the address he didn't need, remembering the exact location.

He was in motion before she finished, Joey and Martin once more following in his wake as he ran all out for the parking lot. They yelled questions at him, but he didn't answer until he was free of the building, dodging groups as he called back, "Get the police to the Russian Orthodox Church. It's an emergency."

Of course with the traffic, it would take them two to three times as long to get there.

Before he slid into his car, his phone rang. It wasn't the Reese woman calling him. The cold calculating voice that sent a fresh wave of fear through him said with a heavy Russian accent, "I have the package you're looking for."

In the background, Aidan heard Bree scream in pain and

his blood ran cold. "You might want to get here before she bleeds out," Vaslov cooed.

His stomach went hollow. "What the fuck do you want?" The man had tortured him, nearly killed Bree the first time. Aidan could only image what he might be doing to her now.

"To watch her bleed to death, but I'm willing to compromise. Bring me Chardy's laptop, and I'll keep her alive until you get here."

I'm going to fucking kill you.

Forcing himself to breathe, Aidan glanced at the backpack on the passenger seat. "I have it and I'm on my way."

***

HONEY POT

"YOU BLEW IT YOU DUMBASS," Bree huffed. The pain was unbearable.

Boris was skilled with knives, and had cut her deeply in multiple places, while in others he simply peeled her skin away. Two of her fingernails were already gone and he was about to start on a third. "The laptop...was in my car. You could have snatched it...if you'd paid attention."

This area of the church was never seen by its parishioners. There were no ornate statues here, no gilded crosses or pictures of saints. It was a sterile room with a sink and drain, a chair and handcuffs. Vaslov, the spy master, was cleaning one of his instruments, Bree's blood washing into the sink. "I already know what is on the laptop."

..de laptop... His accent was harsh in the bare room, and it was all she could do not to give into the pain and fear that hearing it evoked. Those weeks under his control...

Megan, Uncle Martin's assistant, pulled Bree's hair in order to align her upper body with the contraption she was strapping her into. It was one favored by assassins to make a death appear a suicide.

Bree still had fibers from the trunk of the car in her mouth, and spit at Megan. The girl had struck her on the head and stuffed her into the trunk of her car where Bree had come to, briefly, before losing consciousness again. The next time, she was bound and in her current situation and Boris was using his scalpel to wake her up. Thanks to the device, her own hand now held a gun pointed right at her temple.

The whole thing was a decoy. "You're going to kill Aidan," she ground out, resisting Megan's efforts as much as possible.

Boris continued to clean as though he didn't hear her.

Megan laughed, her voice light as if this was a day at Disneyland rather than a torture session. "A murder/suicide. That's what I voted for." She tightened one of the straps, making Bree grunt. "Estranged husband and wife, unable to work out their differences." She tsked. "Such a sad, sad story."

Bree struggled against the restraints, wanting nothing more than to choke the girl. Boris sauntered over. "Careful now, my dear, or you'll end up dead before your husband arrives. We wouldn't want that, now would we?"

He had the audacity to reach out and pat her face. Her injuries were severe, the blood soaking through her clothes, and splashing onto the contraption holding her in the suicide position. The skilled cuts were meant to wound but not kill, and yet she might be dead before Aidan got there regardless. The loss of blood was causing her to feel dizzy and lightheaded. Unconsciousness was only a few breaths away.

Keep him talking. Keep yourself awake. "And the knife wounds?" She blinked through the sweat and blood running into her eyes. "How will the coroner explain the surgical precision?"

Boris smiled and Megan chuckled again, the sound grating on Bree's nerves. "You don't have much imagination, do you? Aidan was a SEAL, for God's sake. He cut you up, you blew his brains out, then in a fit of remorse you killed yourself. The end."

Smartass bitch. Megan was obviously one of the sleeper agents. She'd been right under their nose.

So young and fucking brainwashed, *what a sad, sad story*. "What I may lack in imagination...you lack in brain cells." The girl tightened another strap and it pulled one of the wounds further open, making Bree gasp in pain. Still, she had to get in the taunts while she could. "Vaslov will dispose of you next," she said around the agony. "He's not known for leaving...witnesses."

Megan rolled her eyes, obviously not believing her. Young, brainwashed and *stupid*, Bree added the last one to the list.

Boris stroked the girl's hair, as if he were her lover. "I reward those who do what I tell them."

Reward, right. "So you put Megan at Uncle Martin's spa for what reason?" Bree asked.

Boris smiled. "I needed to take care of some loose ends with the two of you. Megan was there to keep an eye on you, even though you don't make very many family appearances." The knife gleamed as he held it up, examining the blade. "Once I'm done with you and Aidan, I can get back to work on destroying America."

"Aidan's coming for you," Bree hissed, "and your spy ring."

Megan examined her work. "Aidan was a decent guy, and I truly thought I might be able to recruit him to our side. I tried everything! Threw myself at him."

"You were a honey pot." The term was used for a female agent using her wiles to compromise a target.

"Didn't work. He was too in love with you." She poked at a wound and Bree fought back the scream on her lips. "He's a lost cause, but we have bigger fish to fry. Oil rigs, riots by the Mexicans, it's going to be a real party."

Bree could barely stay conscious and fought against the heaviness of her eyelids, the darkness closing in. She had to at least stay awake until Aidan got there, try to warn him.

Boris and Megan kept talking, but their voices drifted, sounding far away. Bree fought to keep herself from passing out.

Have to stay awake...

There was no warning—just *bam*, the door flew open, smacking against the wall and jerking Bree out of her light-headedness.

Aidan stood there, laptop in hand. He'd snuck right up on them, and Boris looked startled, the knife raising as if in defense.

Aidan threw the laptop at Boris's feet. "Let her go."

"Agent McNamara," Vaslov said, regaining his composure "Welcome to the party."

Bree strained, lights dancing at the edges of her vision, threatening to close in no matter how hard she fought. "Aidan... it's a trap. Get out! The laptop was a decoy."

He didn't so much as glance at her, his focus solely on Vaslov. "Last warning. Let. Her. Go."

Megan pulled out a gun and strutted toward him. "No deal. I really liked you," she said. "I wish you didn't have such a boner for her." She waved the gun at Bree.

That was her first mistake, outside of kidnapping Bree to begin with. Aidan moved like a flash of light, and was on top of her in an instant. He grabbed the wrist holding the gun and knocked it sideways.

Megan screamed. The gun fired, plaster falling from the ceiling where the bullet lodged. Aidan disarmed her in another quick movement, knocking her off balance. She stumbled backward, and Boris shifted to the side out of the way, letting her fall.

Everything happened in an instant – Boris threw the knife at Aidan, Aidan went low, kicking out and nailing Boris in the knee. As that happened, Megan tumbled into Bree, nearly knocking her over.

In the next heartbeat, Aidan palmed the knife and threw it at Bree. She closed her eyes and sucked in her breath.

She felt it slice through one of the wires and her hand fell. While the rest of her was still tangled in the straps and pulleys, her arm was now free enough that she could turn the gun on Megan instead.

She didn't hesitate, shooting her in the hip to disable her. Bree tried to fire again, but nothing came out since they only planned on one bullet for her

Click click click, using the last of her strength, she kept trying to shoot Vaslov anyway.

Aidan was taking care of him though. They rolled and fought, Vaslov's weight more than Aidan's, but Aidan's training giving him the upper hand. With a couple swift blows to his head and neck, Aidan disabled Boris, leaving the man unconscious. Maybe dead.

Bree didn't really care at this point, her body giving up as more of her blood drained away and she couldn't stay conscious.

She woke moments later to him releasing her and slapping her face. "Wake up, Bree. You're not checking out on me."

She stared up at him and struggled to do as he said. "I...love you," she whispered. She didn't have the energy for it to be anything more than that.

He must've heard her, and bent so his face was in front of hers. "I've always loved you, and always will. I've never asked you for anything, but today? I'm asking—demanding—this. *Do not die on me.*"

He picked her up and started to carry her out, Bree's arms doing their best to go around his neck and hang on. They'd only gone a couple steps when Aidan suddenly stopped.

"I'm sorry, Bree," a familiar female voice said. "I'm in love with your Uncle Martin, and I didn't want to do this, but now I have no choice. With Boris dead, I guess I'm now in charge."

Bree couldn't believe her ears. She turned her head to see Loretta standing there, holding a gun on her and Aidan.

"You were my mother's...friend. How could you?"

The undercover operative looked sad, truly apologetic, but if Bree had had it in her, she would have jumped Loretta and killed her at that moment. The betrayal stung deeply, the realization that she had trusted her hurt even worse.

Aidan held her tight, taking a step back. "You don't have to take over anything," he said, his voice calm and even. "I can get you a deal. You can get out of this life, build something with Martin, if you really love him. You don't have to do this, Loretta."

She was the last one for them to uncover. All this time, Loretta had been embedded as part of Boris's spy ring. The rage inside Bree reignited adrenaline, and she fought to get out of Aidan's arms, to get to the woman.

Bree knew it before it happened, the change in Loretta's eyes telling her. Aidan must have seen it too, and started to duck and turn to protect Bree.

Using the last of her strength, Bree shoved against him, knocking him off balance as she flipped out of his hold. She heard a bullet fire, the explosion ringing in the room. Megan, still incapacitated, screamed.

Fresh pain tore through Bree's shoulder as she lunged toward Loretta, but the woman was fast, and dodged her grip. Next thing Bree saw was Loretta running away.

"Go after her," Bree yelled at Aidan.

He ignored Loretta, falling to his knees next to Bree. "What the hell was that, Russo?"

The darkness threatened to take her under once more, the feel of Aidan's hands the only reassurance that she'd be okay, whether she lived or died.

"I love you," she repeated.

Seconds before unconsciousness closed in on her, she saw Uncle Martin come into view. In one hand he had Loretta's gun, in the other, he had Loretta.

His face blanched when he saw Bree, but he quipped anyway, "Lose something?"

TEN

T*wenty-four hours later, Sunday night*
Brownsville Hospital

CLANDESTINE OPERATIONS…NOT *for the faint of heart*

AIDAN STOOD AT THE WINDOW, looking out at the darkness. The smell of the hospital was embedded in his skin and nose now, and he longed for a hot shower.

Behind him, soft beeps kept track of Bree's heart rate, the monitors checking her pulse, oxygen intake, and a host of other details. He'd gotten her to the emergency room on the mainland and she'd had surgery, a multitude of stitches, and a dozen different medications to help with pain and keep her from getting an infection. She'd been in and out of it most of the day, and when she had come to, she merely bitched about the pain, the hospital, and anything else she could think of before she fell asleep again.

At least she was getting her spunk back. The knife wounds had not been fatal, of course, since Vaslov wanted her to suffer but appear to have committed suicide. The bastard was dead now, and Aidan was relieved he could never hurt anyone again. Anger still burned in his gut, however, and he would've like to have given the man a taste of his own medicine before he'd killed him.

Megan was talking, spilling her guts in an effort to lessen the charges against her. Loretta, on the other hand, had gone totally silent. She seemed to be old school Russian, refusing to give up any information.

Bree's boss had uncovered the fact that Boris and Loretta had once had an affair, producing Linda. Bree's friend from her younger years had never known who her father was, and now had learned both her mother and father were Russian spies. The shock had to be significant.

The spy ring was going after oil refineries, planning to blow up many of them, and blame it on a Mexican cartel. The rest had been rounded up and were being questioned before they were offered to Russia in exchange for several US operatives being held as political prisoners.

Aidan heard the rustle of sheets. "Where's my wedding band?"

He turned to find Bree awake again, her bandaged hands patting where the necklace had been. Aidan fished it out of his pocket and walked to her, smiling. "Feeling better?"

She took it from him, her skin chilly. "I feel like shit." She removed some of the bandages and slipped the ring on her finger. "But at least Boris is dead, that fucking maniac, although I'd like to bring him back to life and kill him all over again for the scars I'm going to have."

She let go a litany of curses that impressed him, even as a former SEAL.

Smiling to himself, he said, "Beatrice mentioned she'd pay for any plastic surgery you want."

Bree's eyes snapped to his. "You talked to her?"

"I did, and no, I haven't accepted the job. Yet," he added. "I'm not going anywhere until you're back on your feet and we have at least a day or two of normal married life. Although, honestly, I'm not sure either of us knows what that is."

The door burst open and Joey, Candace, and Martin came in, bringing flowers, balloons, and candy, and making over Bree in her bed. She pushed up a little and Aidan helped her get the pillows under her so she was propped up well enough to see and talk to them.

"You're still so pale," Martin said, leaning over and giving her a kiss on the forehead. He was carrying the box of ornaments Aidan had found and set them on the table next to her. "I thought you might want to look through these," he said, winking. "Maybe a little piece of home will make you feel better."

Bree's eyes teared up and she reached for him again. He leaned down and they embraced. When he finally broke away, Bree dashed tears off her cheeks. "I'll take over the spa, Uncle Martin, if Aidan agrees to stay on as security manager."

He and Martin exchanged a knowing look, and the man waved the offer away. "You're a born spy, my dear, and still have work to do to keep this country safe. Your mother would be proud."

He had one of his man bags on and unzipped it. A small Chihuahua head popped out and started panting, a *thump thump thump* coming from inside.

Martin pulled Princess Gracie out and she nearly leapt

from his arms to get to Bree who laughed and embraced her, and the little dog licked her face happily.

Joey and Candace took turns telling Bree about the open house, the now closed florist, and Linda. She seemed to enjoy the gossip, which slightly surprised Aidan, but he was glad of their friendship, something she'd rarely experienced in her life.

After they left, Aidan opened the box. He pulled out a plastic ice skater, wrapped in a red muffler and doing a spin.

Bree's eyes lit up. "I wanted to be a skater when I was seven," she said. "Mom got that for me for Christmas that year." The next was a horse, and again, Bree gave him the details. "That's when I was nine and wanted to be a jockey."

They laughed and she reminisced. Aidan went through several others, each seeming to bring Bree more happiness. He knew she still had to be hurting, but the painkillers were keeping the worst at bay. She smiled, told him a few stories, and laughed more than he'd heard since Vegas.

Even though she was in such banged up shape, she seemed to feel lighter, less burdened down. He hadn't seen that in a long, long time.

She stayed away from talking any more about Boris, Loretta, Megan, and the spy ring, and that surprised him too. She was usually all business, but maybe now, she could find some closure with what had happened to them in Russia. As Aidan put the last ornament back in the box and closed it, he said, "We're going to need a tree to put these on."

Her smile faded and she looked serious. "Aidan, I'll stay here if you want me to. Uncle Martin needs you, and maybe he needs me too." She forced a smile. "I hear the island needs a new florist. How hard can it be to arrange flowers?"

"You have a brown thumb. It'll never work. Your uncle suspected Loretta was a plant, by the way," he told her. "He just didn't know what for."

She shrugged and rolled her eyes. "You can take the spy out of Langley, but you can't take espionage out of the spy, can you?"

They shared a laugh.

Aidan sat on the edge of her bed, taking her hand in his. His fingers found the wedding band and absentmindedly stroked it. It was a good sign she was wearing it again, right? After all they'd been through, the many exchanges of *I love you*, he still wasn't sure.

"So if I want to stay here, keep working for your uncle, you're really okay with that?"

She watched his fingers caressing her ring and she gave him a bright smile. "This spy gig is pretty hard on me," she admitted. "I think maybe I'm ready for a normal life."

Aidan knew better. She'd never been normal in all the time he'd known her, and he doubted she was being truthful with him. "So wherever I go, you're willing to follow?"

She playfully punched him on the arm. "Am I not making myself clear?"

He smiled and dipped his head to kiss her. When he started to pull away, she grabbed him by the back of the neck and kept him there.

The kiss turned hot, like it always did between the two of them, and pretty soon he was laughing against her mouth.

She punched him again, this time not as playfully, and he grunted. "What is so funny?"

Honestly, he wasn't sure, other than just pure happiness. "You're giving up awfully easy."

"Yeah, well, get used to it, at least while I'm on all these drugs."

"I love you, Bree."

"I know. That's why I married you and put up with you all these years."

It was his turn to roll his eyes. "So if I asked you to marry me again, would you do it?"

"Renew our vows?"

He nodded. "Will you marry me again, Bree DeMarco Russo-McNamara?"

"I'll think about it." She smirked. "Okay, I guess so."

He laughed and then went to work kissing her senseless once more.

A*mbush*

AIDAN SAT across from Beatrice Reese in her office. It was plush, but not overly ritzy. The woman herself was direct and no nonsense. She'd made him an offer, and he'd be stupid to refuse it, but he had other things in mind for his future.

"I've uncovered another spy ring and want to go after it."

It'd been a week since Bree had been released from the hospital. Her resolve to stay at the spa with him and her Uncle Martin had lasted approximately six hours. She was supposed to be resting when he found her researching suspicious activity in the Midwest revolving around a known Russian traitor who'd sought refuge in the United States.

Of course, where Bree had gotten the information, he didn't want to know, but he had a strong suspicion the man named Rory had been involved.

Beatrice was quiet, as if waiting for him to continue. He did. "If you want me to work for Shadow Force, you need to send me on missions that play to my strong suits."

She nodded. "I agree."

That was too easy. He suspected Beatrice didn't usually do *easy*. "So we have a deal? I'll work for you, Bree gets her job back, and you let the two of us go after this spy ring she's flushed out in the Midwest."

"Your wife has okayed this plan?"

"She has. Bree insists we team up together and go after it. It's your choice whether we do it for you or someone else."

Beatrice flicked a look at the other woman in the room, Cassandra Donovan. The attorney produced a contract and slid it in front of his face. "I'll need you to sign this."

This was the woman Bree felt responsible for, but she looked pretty healthy to Aidan. He accepted the pen Beatrice handed him and signed without reading it.

"She almost quit because of you," he said in Cassandra's direction.

"I know." She nodded. "None of us were going to let her do that, though. She needed to get her mojo back, and that's why Beatrice sent her to recruit you."

Aidan had the feeling Beatrice knew all about Boris Vaslov and the spy ring he'd been sent to infiltrate and bring down all those years ago.

"Does she know you got her relieved from duty at the CIA?" Reece asked. At his surprised expression, she said, "I've seen your 201."

She'd read his personal CIA file? His gut told him there wasn't much that went on with her employees she didn't know about or have a hand in. He'd spoken to a couple of the other SEALs who worked for her, and he had the strong suspicion they'd been on standby the whole time. A couple were already on the island the night of the open house, ready to provide backup in case Aidan failed.

Good thing he hadn't.

"She suspects," he admitted. "It's another reason I'm working to earn her trust again. I did it to protect her, you know."

"It's what drives people like us." Beatrice motioned between them. "We do what we have to do to protect those we love. Just be sure you come clean to her, and do it soon. I don't want this issue to surface when you're in the field."

I plan to tell her right after her next orgasm. Best to keep that to himself. "I have a lot to make up to her, but I had to get her away from the Agency."

"Her skills are better used for us, so I'm glad you did."

"There's another thing I need from you," he said.

One beautiful eyebrow rose in question.

"Time off for Bree and myself. We don't need a lot," he said, "but it's been a while since we've been on good terms with each other. I want to do something special for her."

For the first time since he'd walked in the door, Beatrice smiled.

BREE WAITED for him in the spacious lobby downstairs. "Well? Did you accept the job?"

She was looking a lot better, her eyes bright, most of the bandages no longer needed, and fewer shadows under her eyes.

"She was absolutely against what I wanted at first," he said, "but I was able to charm my way into getting her to agree to let you and I do what we do best."

He gave her a grin, and she returned it. She seemed

delighted they were going after the Iowa spy ring. "When do we leave?"

"I negotiated a second honeymoon before we head off to the assignment," he said.

"Oh yeah? You were serious about that whole let's get married again thing, huh?"

"Absolutely. I want to renew our vows, start over. A second honeymoon is definitely in order since we spent our first one drunk off our asses."

"Okay. Where are we going?"

He threw an arm around her and lead her to the front doors. "Vegas, Mrs. McNamara. Where else?"

ROMANTIC SUSPENSE & MYSTERIES BY
MISTY EVANS

SEALS of Shadow Force Series: Spy Division

Man Hunt

Man Killer

Man Down

SEALs of Shadow Force Series

Fatal Truth

Fatal Honor

Fatal Courage

Fatal Love

Fatal Vision

Fatal Thrill

Risk

The SCVC Taskforce Series

Deadly Pursuit

Deadly Deception

Deadly Force

Deadly Intent

The Secret Ingredient Culinary Mystery Series

The Secret Ingredient, A Culinary Romantic Mystery with Bonus Recipes

The Secret Life of Cranberry Sauce, A Secret Ingredient Holiday Novella

Paranormal Romance

Witches Anonymous Step 1

Jingle Hells, Witches Anonymous Step 2

Wicked Souls, Witches Anonymous Step 3

Dark Moon Lilith, Witches Anonymous Step 4

Dancing With the Devil, Witches Anonymous Step 5

Devil's Due, Witches Anonymous Step 6

Dirty Deeds, Witches Anonymous Step 7

Wicked Wedding, Witches Anonymous Step 8

Urban Fantasy

Revenge Is Sweet, Kali Sweet Urban Fantasy Series, Book 1

Sweet Chaos, Kali Sweet Urban Fantasy Series, Book 2

Sweet Soldier, Kali Sweet Urban Fantasy Series, Book 3

Sweet Curse, Kali Sweet Urban Fantasy Series, Book 4

USA TODAY Bestselling Author Misty Evans has published fifty novels and writes romantic suspense, urban fantasy, and paranormal romance. She got her start writing in 4th grade when she won second place in a school writing contest with an essay about her dad. Since then, she's written nonfiction magazine articles, started her own coaching business, become a yoga teacher, and raised twin boys on top of enjoying her fiction career.

When not reading or writing, she enjoys music, movies, and hanging out with her husband, twin sons, and two spoiled puppies. A registered yoga teacher and Master Reiki Practitioner, she shares her love of chakra yoga and energy healing, but still hasn't mastered levitating.

Get free reads, all the latest news, and alerts about sales when you sign up for her newsletter at www.readmistyevans.com. To find out more about her holistic healing practice, please visit www.crystalswithmisty.com.

LETTER FROM MISTY

Hello Beautiful Reader!

Thank you for reading this book! It is an honor and a privilege to write stories for you.

I hope you enjoyed this book, and I'd like to ask a favor – would you mind leaving a review at your favorite retailer? I'd really appreciate it, and reviews help other readers find books they will love too.

If you'd like to learn about my other books, sales, and special promotions, please sign up for my newsletter at www.readmistyevans.com.

Grab special edition box sets and get new releases before they come out at retailers by visiting my direct buy website www.mistyevansbooks.com.

I also have a holistic business, Crystals With Misty, and invite you to check out my website www.crystalswithmisty.com for information on my services.

Thank you and happy reading!
Misty

www.ingramcontent.com/pod-product-compliance
Lightning Source LLC
Chambersburg PA
CBHW071015180726
48291CB00004B/1466